UNDERCOVER IN THE DARK

Dark Sons Motorcycle Club - Book Four

ANN JENSEN

Published by Blushing Books
An Imprint of
ABCD Graphics and Design, Inc.
A Virginia Corporation
977 Seminole Trail #233
Charlottesville, VA 22901

Ann Jensen
Undercover In the Dark

eBook ISBN: 978-1-63954-062-4
Print ISBN: 978-1-63954-063-1
v1

Chapter 1

I would give my right tit for a pair of Superman's glasses right now.

One year ago.

A very fingered the gem on her ring nervously. The temptation to hit the panic button was becoming overwhelming. None of her contingencies covered what was happening. She should have been on her way to dinner to arrange a meeting with a new client. A bigger fish than she was used to dealing with. The man was an infamous information broker and human trafficker known as the Recluse. Instead, she was alone in the back of a luxury limousine with three goons who looked at her like she was dinner.

No one knew where she was and her backup was sitting in the restaurant, probably wondering where she was. A year of undercover work and she was only weeks away from the largest take down of her career. What had started as a sting to bring down one of the biggest drug suppliers in Denver might lead to capturing one of the FBI's most wanted. It was that fact that made her hesitate to call for help. If she blew her cover for anything other than to save her life, her supervisors would have her ass.

Avery gestured out the tinted windows. "This is not the way to Nicolo's," she snapped, filling her voice with irritation rather than the genuine fear she felt.

Mateo Lopez and his two men had met her in front of her car near her fake apartment, claiming to need to talk to her before the meeting. She'd had little choice but to get into the limo with them.

"Mr. Thomas had an opening in his schedule, so we are going to meet him now." Mateo's smile wasn't comforting.

"You said the meeting was next week. I have none of the information I need with me." More importantly, she didn't have a swarm of DEA and FBI agents waiting in the wings, ready to arrest the man.

Mateo's chuckle was mocking. "I am sure you'll be fine. After all, Ms. Garcia, it's no different from the work you've been doing for years. Correct?"

"I don't appreciate surprises. Up to now, our business has been extremely lucrative for both of us. What I do takes time and planning. If Mr. Thomas can't be patient, then I have no interest in working with him."

"Oh, he's a very patient and well-connected man."

The view of the city disappearing into highway outside the limo's windows made it clear they were leaving Denver. Avery knew she needed to do something soon if she had any hope of salvaging the situation.

"That may be but I've been very clear I only meet in venues of my choosing." She gestured out the window. "I don't do business like this. Have your driver drop me off. I'll call a car for myself. If Mr. Thomas wants to work with me, he has to follow the same rules as everyone else."

"Your money laundering skills are amazing. Almost too good to be true." Mateo pulled a gun from his holster by his side.

She pressed down on the gem in her ring, activating the panic button. Help would come, but it would probably be too late.

"That is completely unnecessary." She nodded at his gun. "There is no such thing as too good in my business. I am careful and I don't get caught, that's why you hired me." Staying calm with a gun pointed at her and two thugs on either side was hard.

For the last year, she had pretended to be the daughter of a dead cartel member. The DEA had made sure they protected her at all times as she wined and dined drug and gunrunners. She had stayed cool with each encounter because she had the safety net of backup. Threats, lewd suggestions, none of it had bothered her. Here in the back of this limo, all of that bravado failed her. Her stomach twisted as predictions of what could happen to her flickered through her mind.

Hatred blazed out of Mateo's eyes. "I hired you because your references were impeccable. You never asked questions and always delivered what you promised."

"Then why the theatrics?" Avery said through gritted teeth.

"Mr. Thomas is more connected than I am. He was disappointed to find out that the FBI knew all about our transactions. In fact, he found out exactly who you are, Agent Perez."

Fear turned to terror as she realized she wasn't just in danger of being exposed, they had blown her cover wide open. That it was a leak in the FBI was a bitter pill. Bringing them in to the case last month had been a risk. Undercover operations could be exposed with a single wrong word, but so close to the end her superiors had thought the extra help was worth the risk. A poor decision she was going to pay for with her life.

Avery kicked out, the heel of her shoe catching Mateo in the wrist with the point of the stiletto. She tried to reach for her own gun, but the two men sitting next to her grabbed her arms. She was well trained by the DEA and an expert in several martial arts since childhood. None of that would overcome the disadvantage of the small space or the size difference of the large men attacking her. Even knowing it was pointless, she struggled, bit, and clawed at the men trying to hold her down. Only when they had her pinned face down on the seat with a knee in her back, did she finally give in to the inevitable.

"If you kill a federal agent, there will be nowhere you can hide." Tears of frustration pricked at her eyes, but there was no way she would let them see them.

"Oh, they will look for you, bitch. You're a dirty agent who shot her partner, stole millions and took off with her Russian lover. You might even make their most wanted list." Mateo's words were like ice against her spine.

"What the fuck are you talking about?" She bucked against the man who pinned her down.

"We've known who you are for a month. Setting you up was child's play. Besides, killing you is too easy. No one betrays me and gets a painless death."

"You shot Nate?" Her partner had been a gentle man, not really suited for the line of work they were in. No one would believe she had turned on him. They had been friends almost since she graduated from training and started with the DEA. Had they really killed him? She didn't want to picture a world without her partner's easy laugh and corny jokes.

"Not personally. But he is dead. I paid Mr. Thomas a pretty penny to make sure the evidence will show you did it. I'm going to enjoy watching everyone turn against you."

She bucked up against the man holding her down. "You bastard!"

"I'm going to enjoy breaking you. Me and my men are going to spend days making you pay for your betrayal. The beauty of it, if there is enough of you left when we get bored, Mr. Thomas will make a profit off of selling you to someone who will enjoy you no matter how broken."

Bile rose in her throat. She shook her head. There was no way she would let this asshole break her. She would find a way to make them all pay.

Chapter 2

We walk in the darkness so you can enjoy the light.

"Fuck, I always forget how hot this fucking gear is."

Max looked over at his Brother Ink and rolled his eyes at Rooster's whining. The team of twenty men from Dark Sons Motorcycle Club were all decked out in the same gear. Black cargo pants and Henley shirts with Kevlar vests, helmets, and face masks to protect both their bodies and identities. The mission they were on was righteous, if not legal.

A nasty piece of shit called the Recluse had held Sharp's old lady, Pixie, prisoner. He was a man so bad he was on the blacklist of every alphabet agency. Back when Max had still been an Agency man, even he had tried to find the fucker. So using her information to raid his properties was karmic justice. What he did to women, what had happened to her, was the stuff of nightmares.

Pixie had handed them the info they needed to rid the

world of this asshole, and they would not hesitate. There was no red tape, no bullshit, or hidden agendas. That was just one of a hundred reasons he had faked his own death and signed up to become a Dark Son. The unflinching dedication of every man standing outside the warehouse, ready to end this asshole, validated his choice once again.

"I've got eyes inside," Tek said over their coms. "Twenty-two hostiles roaming ground level. Five hostiles in the basement with over twenty lambs. Bravo Plan in thirty seconds on my mark."

Hawk, their president, raised his arm and began the count. The door blew open and his unit moved. Through the back and off to the left, where the stairs to the basement were. Gunfire sounded in the distance, but Max stayed focused.

One man exited the top of the stairwell and his and Ink's bullets put the man down before he even saw them coming. Easing down the stairway, Ink was in the lead. The short hallway they entered was like some strange version of an asylum. Graying sidewalls held four padlocked doors with observation windows. The end of the hall had a double door that looked to be barred from this side.

Each window gave a horrible view into Hell. Naked, bruised, and terrified women huddled on cement floors. Max clenched his teeth, wanting to free these women now but knowing they needed to clear the enemy first.

"Fucking Hell." Ink's curse had Max on high alert. The Texan was creative in his language, but rarely allowed an actual curse word to escape. Leaning to the side, he gazed into the room at the end of the hall.

The space displayed through the small windows was much larger than the cells they had passed. Shackled to the center of the floor by a chain was a naked woman covered in bruises. Unlike the other women in the cells, she didn't look defeated. Instead, she crouched in a fighting stance, almost daring someone to attack her. Four hostiles circled just outside her reach, using pool cues to strike at her. No sound came through the door, but the smiles on the men's faces said they were laughing.

The woman had a feral beauty and grace to her movements. Her red hair whipped around her as she turned with a snarl clear in her face. If she wasn't chained in place, Max didn't doubt she would do some damage before they ever laid a hand on her.

"I'm gonna open this door on three," Ink drawled. "Max and Hannibal, you take out the trash."

Max shouldered his weapon, ready and eager to follow his Brother's command. The doors swung open and allowed them to both surprise the occupants and to enter two by two. The sound of their rifles in the small room was loud and echoed but within seconds four men were bleeding out on the floor.

It would have been more satisfying to take their time and make the scum suffer, but unfortunately vengeance wasn't the purpose of the day. Safety of the victims and finding the man behind the operation was.

"Zone three clear heading to Zone one," Ink's Texan drawl came from behind Max.

"Zone two clear lambs secure." Gear's calm words echoed over the coms.

"Zone four clear minor casualties."

"Zone one is still hot. Three hostiles remain in the northern quadrant, one lamb." Sharp's voice was tight followed by an explosion. Long seconds passed. "Zone one clear."

Max let out his breath, confident that all he had to worry about was the mess in front of him. The room was clear of hostiles and had no other entrances. The woman, crouched on the floor, had picked up one of the pool cues her abusers had been using. He had to admire her tenacity in finding a weapon even while chained naked in the middle of a gunfight.

Max slung his weapon to his back and tried to look less aggressive. "It's okay, wildcat. You're safe." He held up his hands to try to calm her. Her gorgeous eyes were wide with the instinct to fight. As beautiful as her wild defiance was, she would need to settle if they were going to get her safe.

"You secure and calm her down, we'll free the others." Hawk's deep voice filled the room.

Max didn't take his eyes off the beauty in front of him, knowing she was unpredictable in this heightened state of fight or flight. He nodded and heard his Brothers step out of the room.

"Who the hell are you?" The woman's voice was scratchy and deep, as if she'd hurt it by screaming.

"We're the good guys."

She snorted. "Good guys don't wear black combat fatigues with no markings and hide behind face masks."

It was tempting to flip up the face shield to put her at ease, but it wasn't just his safety he would be risking. "Today we're the good guys." Max took a step forward.

She jumped back, wincing but held her weapon steady. He stopped, not wanting her to hurt herself more.

"Stay back or I'll take your dick off," she snarled.

Her resistance shouldn't be hot, but it was. Bruised and chained to the floor by her ankle she still radiated danger. Her muscles clenched to fight showed, despite her lush curves, she was no weakling. She was a warrior ready to do battle. He had to respect the strength it took for her not to back down.

Max smiled. On the wall to his right, he saw a keychain hung on a hook. "I'm sure you'd try." He walked over and grabbed the keys. "How about I unchain you?"

Her eyes narrowed, and she nodded. She shifted her stance so her chained ankle was forward. Max walked over and found the right key. The snick of the lock was a welcomed sound.

Her muscles tensed and gave him just enough warning to block the blow aimed for his head. The helmet would have absorbed most of the hit, but he wasn't taking any chances. Max swept his arms behind her knees, knocking her off balance and tumbling to the floor.

He had to scramble to catch her before her head had an unfortunate meeting with the concrete. He might not be willing to take a blow, but he didn't want her to have to suffer more injuries. Pain shot up his arm. The devious minx bit him! Max flipped her over, using his body weight to pin her face down to the ground.

She bucked and wiggled under him, causing his body to react in completely inappropriate ways. He loved the struggle for dominance between a man and a woman. The more violent the struggle, the better, but only if both parties were having fun. Unfortunately, his dick wasn't as picky as his brain and was now hard as steel.

"Problems?" Hannibal's Louisiana twang was filled with amusement.

Max gripped the woman by the hair and used all his weight to pin her motionless. "The wildcat here doesn't seem to understand this is a rescue."

She tried to buck him off but only managed to grind her naked, plump ass temptingly against his cock.

"You've got your dick rubbing against my ass like a hopped up Chihuahua and I'm supposed to be grateful?"

"You need help with that filly?" Ink's Texas drawl let him know the annoying duo were witnessing his struggles.

"No, I'm good." His words were bitten out through clenched teeth.

Hannibal's laughter did nothing for his temper. The fight to keep this professional was getting harder. His mind and body fighting over what to do. He kept his emotions under tight lock down because when he let loose people got hurt.

She kicked her feet and squirmed. Enough was enough. He smacked her ass, hard.

"If I wanted to hurt you, you'd be hurt," he growled into her ear. "You need to get yourself settled Wildcat or I'm going to tie you up like a goose on Thanksgiving."

"My name is not Wildcat." She stopped struggling, but Max was still wary.

"What is it then?"

"None of your business."

Hannibal and Ink chuckled. Max had to respect her spunk. God only knew what she had been through before they got here. It settled something inside him to know they had saved this bright soul from being broken.

Max eased up his grip a bit. "Okay, Wildcat, if I let you up, are you going to keep fighting or are you going to behave and join the other women so we can figure out how to get you back home?"

"You're letting us go?" The shock in her voice hurt, but he couldn't really blame her.

"We are."

"You swear?"

"I do."

"Then I'll behave." The words sounded like they came out of gritted teeth. Max laughed. He slowly got off of her, ready for another attack.

The battered, naked woman stood with the dignity of a queen, her chin held high. She was his darkest fantasy come to life. Red hair like a wild crown around her head. Naked and alone in a room with three strange men, she showed no fear.

He had never been more tempted to go back on his word. He wanted to keep her all for himself.

Chapter 3

It's funny how sometimes the people you'd take a bullet for are the ones behind the trigger.

A very had been wrong when she thought she'd seen the worst of humanity. The shivering, broken wrecks of the women prisoners huddling at the edges of the room were nothing she could have dreamed. Bile was bitter in the back of her throat. Her nightmares would get an upgrade that night.

How long would it have been before she would have broken? Pride said weeks, but a scared part of her wondered if she could have lasted that long. From the bruises and cuts covering their bodies, Avery didn't want to think of the systematic torture and rape these women had endured.

She had only been beaten and captured for a few hours, yet already she knew she would have trouble. The thought of letting someone grab her wrists or getting into the back of a car with someone left her cold. The journey back from wherever these women had gone mentally was going to be a longer and bumpier ride.

The men walking around in their black BDUs and skull face masks didn't appear to be any form of law enforcement. Functioning as a unit, they had gotten the victims gathered into the main room. Something about the way they moved and carried their weapons screamed ex-military to Avery. The way they flawlessly worked together meant they weren't strangers brought together quickly. Could they be mercenaries?

Why had they attacked this place and freed her? They were stern with the captives but not abusive or abrasive. They obviously were looking for something. Men carried out computers and boxes to white vans, that had no license plates, in a steady stream.

The intent was obviously to empty the place of all evidence. Even the dead bodies were being taken away. The part of her that was an agent snarled at the obvious cover-up. Would they get rid of the witnesses with the same precision they got rid of everything else?

No.

Their rescuers carried their illegal weapons like professionals and treated the women with dignity. They had found clothing or at least sheets for each of the prisoners to cover up with. Who would have thought learning to wrap a toga for her high-school play would be so useful someday? As she helped the women get dressed in the makeshift garments, hope solidified in her chest that these men really meant to release them.

It didn't stop her from trying to pick up every clue she could about the mystery men. So far she had noticed several of the men, including the man she wrestled with downstairs, had scruffy beards sticking out beneath their facemasks. They were also ridiculously in-shape, and many had tattoos on what little skin was visible. Their artwork was quality, not prison grade, but so far she hadn't seen enough to positively identify anyone later.

One man was giving them all water bottles. Avery checked to make sure it hadn't been tampered with before chugging down the liquid.

A chill went up her spine as another man in black entered the room. She would have recognized his confident stride and dangerous grace even if the beard and light blue eyes hadn't given him away. This was the man who had pinned her so easily in the basement. The memory of his big frame holding her down shouldn't have excited her. But she couldn't deny wanting a second chance to wrestle, maybe with him naked as well.

"What's the plan?" His voice held anger that Avery understood. He pushed up his sleeves as if ready to fight. On his right arm was probably the most beautiful tattoo she had ever seen. A motorcycle so realistic, the colors so vibrant, it looked like it might drive right off his muscled forearm.

The other man turned to face him. "Clean's crews already have the bodies and we aren't bothering with anything else. We found money, computers, and enough prescription drugs to start our own pharmacy but Tek says there is no sign of Mitchel at either location."

Was Clean or Tek one of these men's call sign? Avery knew enough military men to know they often had ridiculous nicknames. She stored that and the other information for later.

"And the girls?" the one with the cool tattoo asked.

"Any of them sane enough to call the cops after we're long gone?"

Not wanting to miss an opportunity at more information, she stood up. "I can."

The blue eyes of the man she had fought locked with hers. His gaze roamed her body, and she might have blushed if the situation wasn't so crazy. He had seen her completely naked earlier, but it felt like his gaze was roaming up and down her makeshift outfit like he was trying to see underneath. He reached his gloved hand into his pocket and pulled out a cellphone.

He was going to give her a way to call for help, just like that? Maybe she had misread these men. Would criminals care if these women had a way to call for help?

"Screen's locked but you can hit the emergency call after we've left." His voice was a growl, as if he was trying to put a threat into the last few words.

Crazy thoughts raced through her mind. She didn't want this sexy hero to be a bad guy. Maybe they were undercover FBI or some other organization trying to take down this organization but not wanting to be recognized. If they were connected to law enforcement, then they would have been briefed on her cover and maybe told she might be here.

"I'm Trisha," she gave her cover name, hoping one of them would slip and give her more information. Maybe if she put on the helpless girl vibe, they would slip and tell her their names. She did her best to put an apology for her earlier attack into her eyes. He raised an eyebrow as if calling bullshit on her sweet act, but she just smiled.

The first man spoke up, breaking their staring contest. "Wait as long as you can—an hour would be great, but ten minutes is enough if you can't."

Avery nodded. Mr. Blue-eyes spun away, shook his head and left her with his buddy. She needed to know if she was dealing with criminals or law enforcement. She cleared her throat and clutched onto the phone. "Can I ask you something?"

"You can ask." The look in the man's eyes said clearly he wouldn't be answering anything he didn't want to.

"Are you guys FBI?" she asked more to see his reaction.

The man burst out laughing, and she had her answer. These guys were criminals who had no respect for the law. She glared at him, and he reeled it in. "No. Just concerned citizens."

He strolled away from her, still chuckling under his breath. Well, screw them. The sounds of their motorcycles and cars pulling away was like a trigger to the over twenty women huddling in the room. Soon they were crying and rocking like wounded animals. She couldn't wait an hour. Hell, she couldn't even wait five minutes. These women needed help now.

The sound of sirens filled Avery with relief. Selfish as it was, she needed to hand the responsibility for keeping all these women safe and contained to someone else. When one had tried to run off naked, the temptation to let her go had almost been overwhelming. She was strong, but the events of the day had used up all her energy.

The set of police sweats she had been given helped her feel more at ease. Without that small comfort, she didn't think she would have been able to get through all the questions. She had run through the details of what had happened several times already and guessed it would be a hundred or more times before the questions stopped.

Any time they paused the interrogation, Avery asked again if they had any information on her partner or when anyone from the DEA would show up. She had tried calling Nate on one of the officer's phones, but much to her dismay no one answered. Dread was settling in her stomach that the bastard Mateo had been telling the truth, and her partner was dead.

"Avery Perez?" A clipped male voice called from behind her.

"Yes." She turned to see a man in an FBI windbreaker.

He reached out to grab her arm, and she stepped back.

"What the hell?" She couldn't deal with anyone touching her right now. The bruises from earlier still throbbed in time with her pulse, and she was barely holding it together after her adrenaline started to drop when the police arrived.

"You are under arrest for the murder of Nathan Chatham." The man gripped her wrist and tried to twist it behind her back.

Something snapped inside her, and she lashed out. This couldn't be happening. She couldn't let them cuff her. Had to break free. She wouldn't be a prisoner again. A haze dropped over her eyes and she kicked, feeling her bare foot impact with the person trying to chain her up.

Shouts bounced off her ears as she twisted out of the grip of another person trying to pin her down. What were they doing! How dare they attack her?

A primal scream ripped out of her throat as she charged the nearest of her attackers. Pain like viscous ice tore through her body as her muscles lost control.

A taser.

She tried to move, but blows rained down on her, each hurt melting into the next. She had to escape. She had to!

Chapter 4

"When I'm good, I'm very good. But when I'm bad I'm better" –
Mae West

Present Day

Max sat at the Clubhouse bar, sipping his scotch and trying to relax. It was Friday afternoon. And he was looking forward to the distraction the party that night would provide. His mission to see every one of the women they had rescued from the Recluse's compound taken care of was almost over. He had spent the last year making sure each woman was safe and hopefully on the path to healing. All except one.

Trisha, the hellcat from the basement, had vanished without a trace. Records were clear; the police had been called as soon as they had left. He had to assume that was her. Somewhere between the phone call and the police arriving she had vanished. The police had no record of her or anyone matching her description being brought to the hospital. He had spent more fruitless nights trying to search for Trisha than he was comfortable admitting. Finding the last, and most interesting, of the captives had become an obsession.

He needed to find her. This mission had to be a success. During the years he had worked for the black side of the government, there had been too many compromises that had left his soul stained. Ensuring those women got the help and support they needed wouldn't clear his debt to the world, but it helped lift the weight of guilt.

Helping while remaining anonymous wasn't easy. In some cases, he had found their families after the lazy fucks in the government gave up. Others he set up in rehab using a charity to front his actions. And in one or two cases, he sent them to a deprogramming expert he knew in Texas, in the hopes he could help them find their way back to whoever they had been before the brainwashing and abuse they had endured.

But his Wildcat, she was a mystery. He didn't have any sort of idea of who Trisha had been, or where she'd gone. It was driving him insane. It wasn't like he needed her for himself.

He didn't have to talk to her. Or wrestle with her again. Max definitely shouldn't do any of the things his dirty mind slipped into his dreams several nights a week. But he had to know she was okay. Hell, she probably would want nothing to do with him if he found her, but he couldn't let it go.

"Hey, Daddio. Nice wig chop." The woman's voice came from behind him. He spun, trying to find the source of the odd words.

Standing there in one of the most ridiculous outfits he'd ever seen was Cami, his Brother Tek's Old Lady. Her purple hair was up in a high ponytail. And she wore a collared white sweater. With, he swore to God, a poodle skirt flaring out from under it. He looked down at her feet and, yes, she had on saddle shoes. He was glad his Brother was happy, but his old lady was one step away from the loony bin.

She was the only person here who had known him before he had faked his own death to escape the nightmare that had been his life. Their chance encounter a few months ago had thrown him for a loop. She brought up memories he preferred to forget. To his shame, he had tried to run her off when they met again.

But his Brother Tek's crazy had matched hers perfectly and now the two were sickeningly happy. Both got off on the strange role playing she seemed to pop into and out of at a moment's notice. More power to them. Who was he to complain about his Brother finding his happy?

Max raised an eyebrow. "Wig chop? What the hell is that, sweetie?" He tried to remember not to treat her like a child but to him she would always be the spunky teen hacker he had first met.

She waved her hand around her head. "Haircut? You know? You're all shaved and your hair's short. When did you decide to get rid of the wild man look?"

Max ran his hand through his now short hair. After the wild ride to the hospital a few weeks ago to help his Brother Sharp's Old Lady Pixie deliver her baby, he had a wake-up call. The image of a small child at the hospital clinging to his mom's leg after getting a look at him stuck in his thoughts.

He really didn't give a shit what anybody thought about his appearance. But when his beard and hair were so scary, small children had to be carried away from you crying in fear it was time to get to the barber.

"It was time for a change." He shrugged. No reason to over share.

She cocked her head as if not believing him, but let it go. "I'm glad I caught you before Tek and I went out for a ride."

Cami pulled a file out from the messenger bag slung across her shoulder and tossed it up onto the bar top. "Sorry, it took me so long. But you know with Pixie going into labor and everything. I forgot for a few days. But there's the info on your girl."

It took Max a few seconds to remember Cami had offered to help with his search for the mystery woman. He grabbed the file and flipped it open. Pictures and pages of printouts filled the folder.

"You found her?" He shouldn't be surprised, but he was. Staring out from the photos was the woman he had been searching for. Different hair colors and clothing styles, looks so different that you wouldn't know they were the same person if you didn't look closely enough.

"Yeah. I'm not sure you should keep looking for her." Cami bit her lip as if debating about saying something.

Max looked up from the pictures and gave her his full attention. He would spend the night studying the contents, but she had already read it all. Learning whatever she thought was important now would be helpful.

"Tell me what you know about Trisha."

"Well, f-first thing is her n-name's not Trisha."

Cami had a stutter that intensified when she was stressed or in large social situations. It's appearance now meant he really needed to know what she was hesitating over.

"Okay. I know that is what she said but it could have been a nickname." In less than a week she had found more than Tek, and the several other people he had looking into it had discovered in the last year. "How did you find all this?"

"You k-know, I've got my sources." She shrugged. "Trisha Garcia is a cover identity. T-there is a giant fake history in Mexico. But everything she did here in the States is all shadowy and had to be pulled out of some of the darker places that I search."

"Mexico?" Max held off on asking about her real identity,

trying to puzzle out something. Cover identities were usually created for a reason, and that could help him figure her out.

"Yeah."

"She's got the look. But she isn't from there." Max tried to place his finger on what felt off. He remembered their fight. And everything about that time in the basement. The woman hadn't had an accent. Usually in stressful situations, whatever your birth accent was, comes out in force. She also hadn't cursed at him in Spanish. In his experience, people under stress cursed in their native language.

"No, she's from New J-Jersey."

"So you found her real identity?"

The eye roll she gave him was cute. "Yeah, Avery Perez. Ex-DEA agent. She w-worked in the same office as Agent D-Devin."

Max understood now why Cami was so nervous. Agent Devin had been the SOB who had made her life hell for years. The fact that he had died recently in a car wreck hadn't lessened her dislike of the man.

"You said ex?"

Cami reached into the file and pulled out a printout of a web news story and handed it to him. The headline read: *Mountain Murderess on the Loose.*

Max scanned the article. Her jailbreak during transport had left two guards injured. A fuzzy unrecognizable mug shot of Avery with orange-blonde hair was included. It described that she was accused of killing her partner as well as two inmates. She had been in the process of being transported to a maximum-security prison when the van had engine trouble and she had managed to escape.

Something was off with the article. Max had plenty of experience with cover ups. This reeked of that. The details gory enough to satisfy the public but lacking any real depth.

"Could this be another cover?"

Cami shook her head. "Everyone wants her dead though they are pretending to try and capture her."

The article was dated over a month ago. "And they don't have any leads?"

"Nope. I think hunting her down was one of the things Agent Devin w-wanted me to d-do." She wrung her hands and Max felt guilty for dredging up bad memories.

He reached over and squeezed her hand. While it was tempting to keep pushing and get every piece of information he could on Avery, she was obviously uncomfortable. He would study what she had already given him before pushing for more.

"Thanks for doing this. I'll look this over and take it from here." Max smiled and changed the subject. "So what do you and Tek have in mind for tonight? I'm trying to figure out how big poofy skirts and sweaters fit into some sort of kink."

Cami smiled and twirled in her skirt. "Max, you don't want to know what kind of dirty things a bad boy is gonna do with a good girl tonight after he takes her to the malt shop for an ice cream."

Max chuckled, glad she wasn't looking nervous anymore. He held up his hands. "You're right. But thanks again for this."

After she skipped off, Max read the file poring over the details. The more he read, the more things didn't match up. He had only met her the once but that brave vibrant woman was not the kind of coward that would shoot her partner in the back in cold blood.

He studied the evidence gathered against her for trial. On the surface it was bulletproof. The timeline was odd. If this was right, she would have barely had enough time to kill her partner then end up chained in that basement. The prosecution was claiming she was hiding out with the slaver before fleeing the country but had left the murder weapon in her apartment. The accounts that held her dirty money were too easily found. All of it was just too perfect.

Evidence, in his experience, was nothing like on TV. It was messy and hard to get. Leaps of logic were necessary, along with a touch of luck, which would often take investigators months to put together to have enough evidence for court. In less than a week, these detectives had collected enough concrete proof to put her away for life.

Something was off.

Did he care if she was a dirty agent? Yeah, he had worked with too many of those in his career. Back then he hadn't known better or had a choice. Taken straight out of Marine bootcamp into ops so black he hadn't known who he was working for half the time. Young and dumb, he had almost lost his soul to those assholes.

He needed to know the truth about his Wildcat before he could even think of stopping his search.

Chapter 5

If you can't see the light at the end of the tunnel just light that bitch up yourself

Avery sat gathering her thoughts in the midafternoon sunlight in the front seat of her crappy stolen car. The tattoo parlor in front of her was the last one on her list for Colorado, but she tried not to get her hopes too high. She took a moment to look herself over in the mirror and barely recognized herself after the last month on the run. She had changed in so many ways. It wasn't her hair, which was now back to her natural dark brown or the weight she had dropped while on the run. It was the tightness in her features, which were the result of the many moral lines she had crossed to stay alive and free.

Being an undercover agent had given her the skills she needed to survive. Had you asked her a year ago if she would break into a federal prosecutor's house to steal a case file or rob multiple drug houses to get the money she needed to survive, she would have laughed. Now those were just a few of the crimes she had committed.

Kidnapping and torturing the truth out of the FBI agent who, she was pretty sure, had set her up, was starting to look like a viable plan. If she couldn't find her mystery rescuers, and if she couldn't get the information she needed from them, it might be her only option. Hiding forever, letting the assholes who had set her up get away with it, wasn't in her DNA. Stupidly, at first, she had trusted the system. Four attempts on her life and two dirty transport guards intent on raping and killing her had destroyed that optimism.

Dark Ink was the last place on her list of tattoo shops in Colorado who could have done the hyper realistic artwork she had seen on the men who had rescued her. Even a year later, every detail of the tattoo on blue eyes' arm was fresh in her mind. If she found him then she might find the evidence she needed to clear her name of her partner's murder. Hope was all she had.

Avery swung her legs out of her car onto the pavement, pulling up her thigh-high boots before standing. A 1% Motorcycle club that had its hands in everything, both legal and illegal, ran Dark Ink. Her outfit had been carefully picked to play into the stupid, sexist stereotypes those kinds of men expected. Women were arm candy, only good for sex. So her skirt was short, her makeup heavy, and her top tight.

If this was the right place she would have to convince them to give her the name of the man with the tattoo and men loved to brag to women they wanted to fuck.

The shop wasn't what she expected on the inside. White, black and chrome it was a clean and modern vibe with just a hint of retro. The color in the place came from large photographs of gorgeous people with tattoos covering their bodies.

Excitement bubbled in her stomach as she thought she recognized the style. A few of the artists looked up from their stations when she walked in, but quickly went back to work. The hot factor for the men both working and getting tattoos was crazily high. A bored young woman with tattoos crawling up her neck and onto her face sat reading a magazine at the front desk. If this girl was more than a few months over eighteen, she would eat her boots. Avery's luck with women wasn't nearly as good as it was with men, but she approached the desk with a smile.

"Hi!" She kept her tone light and bubbly. "I'm thinking about getting a tattoo. Can you help me?"

The girl looked up with a raised eyebrow. "Let me guess. You want a flower or dolphin on your ankle."

"No." Avery tried not to let her annoyance at the snotty comment show. She stepped to the side of the desk and leaned forward as if sharing a secret, making sure the position displayed both her ass and cleavage to anyone looking. "I want, like a super realistic motorcycle. You have anyone who does work like that here?"

"Yeah, but he has a nine month waiting list for new customers." The receptionist was obviously unimpressed by her act but as expected, Avery noticed several of the men checking out her ass.

"Oh, I'm willing to wait if the person is skilled enough. I'd love to see the work and maybe talk to the artist to get an idea of what they can do." She shifted her weight a bit and felt the fabric of her skirt riding a little higher.

A male chuckle from behind her let her know she was having the desired effect. "Let her look at Ink's book, Gia."

The man's velvet smooth Louisiana accent sounded familiar. Avery looked back over her shoulder to see a gorgeous black man staring hungrily at her ass. He sat with a tattoo gun in one hand and his phone in the other. The artist wore the black vest that men like him called a cut. Obviously one of the Dark Sons who ran this place.

She winked. "Thanks."

His eyes flared with what she assumed was interest before she turned back around. Perfect, she had a possible in to their Club if it turned out she needed more information.

The girl at the desk looked surprised, but shrugged. "Sure, Boss." She reached under the counter and pulled out a photo book almost three inches thick and flipped pages using a tab. "These are some of the motorcycles he's done. You can look at them over there."

The woman nodded to some comfortable looking black leather chairs against the wall. Excited, Avery nodded her thanks and took the book to sit down. She'd looked through so many tattoo books over the last month that she shouldn't get her hopes up, but something inside her said she was about to finally get a clue.

Some of the ink in the photos was so impressive it was hard to believe they weren't photos. She flipped a few pages and barely contained her whoop of excitement as a photo of the very tattoo she dreamed about was displayed across the page. All her work was about to pay off. She would get the identity of the sexy forearm in the photo no matter what.

"Got your text, Hannibal. You need help with something? I was about to take off for the Clubhouse." The Texas drawl pulled her back in time.

You need help with that filly?

She wrenched herself out of the memory, knowing now that she was definitely in the right place. The man standing next to the well-muscled and tattooed black man who had been checking out her ass was the picture of bad-boy cowboy. Despite the ink that covered his body and his Dark Sons cut, he still exuded an almost wholesome country vibe. Shaggy blond hair and a face made for smiling, he probably had women lining up at his door. She preferred a rougher cut of man, but she could appreciate the appeal.

Hannibal nodded to his phone, then at her. For a moment she thought they might recognize her. "Nah. Got a potential customer for you."

This must be Ink. It was an obvious nickname for a tattoo artist. She wondered what the story was behind Hannibal's nickname. Was he a cannibal or something? The cowboy tattoo artist gave her a saucy wink before looking down at his friend's phone. He gave a broad smile that was almost feral.

She wondered if Hannibal had snapped a picture of her ass on display. Men only got that look before sex or violence, and she wasn't up for either.

He strolled over to her with a predatory glide and looked down at the page she held open in her lap. "Not many women want a tattoo quite so gritty."

It took her mind a minute to kick into gear. She couldn't blow this chance. The pieces fell into place. If these two had been part of the men who rescued her, then they would have access to the information she needed. Rumor was that all the Dark Sons members were ex-military. The men that day had acted as a unit. Was it possible she had a motorcycle club to thank for saving her and all those women?

"I like it. It's sort of primal and modern at the same time."

He chuckled. "It's one of the bikes from *"Mad Max"*. You ever see the movie?"

Had she, please, she loved the classics. "I hope you're talking *"Beyond Thunderdome"* because the others aren't tattoo worthy."

"Well, aren't you just a surprise?" He smiled. "Come on back and we'll get you set up."

Wait. What?

"I thought you had a waiting list." Was she going to actually get a tattoo? She loved the look of tattoos, especially this man's work, but had always avoided getting one. Identifying marks when you were undercover were a no-no.

"I had the afternoon off, but for you I'll make an exception." His eyes roamed her body with an amused twinkle.

"Oh. And it'll be just like that one?" she asked. The man behind the tattoo had haunted her fantasies for way too long. How she could find a man attractive – whom she had never really seen – was baffling. Unfortunately, her dreams had been filled with alternate endings to their wrestling match. Ones that left her wet and aching.

"I can do that. Where do you want it?" His voice held a hint of a dare, like he expected her to back out.

She wouldn't back down. Where could she put it that clothes would cover it, but she could still enjoy looking at it? The idea of having a matching tattoo with the man she had been hunting for the last month had excitement building in her core.

"My hip."

He raised an eyebrow. "Sensitive spot, think you can handle it?"

"Oh, I can handle anything you can dish out." It probably wasn't the smartest response. She was trying to make him think she was harmless. Sometimes the fire she had inherited from her mother slipped out.

"I'm sure you can." He shook his head. "What's your name, sweetness?"

Biting back her instinct to rail against the crappy endearment, she gave a smile that probably held too many teeth. "Cat. You can call me Cat."

It was probably stupid playing off the nickname they had given her. But this man was so focused on her assets she doubted he would recognize her, even if she still had the red hair and fifteen extra pounds cushioning her body.

"All right, Cat. The tattoo will take at least two sessions but we can lay down the outline today."

Putting back on her ditzy persona, she pushed a bit. "I won't mind two sessions with you. Any way I could see the other tattoo in person? The picture's great but it would be so cool if I could see what the color's going to look like in person."

He offered her a hand up from the chair, and she took it. Avery gave him what she hoped was a seductively pleading look, and his lip twitched in a smile.

"I think that can be arranged."

Finally, things were starting to go right for her. She would find her way into their little boys' club and get the information she needed to clear her name.

Chapter 6

If the words don't add up, it's usually because the truth wasn't included in the equation.

Max growled as he kicked down the jiffy stand of his Harley. Two hours. Two fucking hours since he had received the text from Hannibal that upended his day.

Hannibal: *We found your girl.*

The picture attached had been a gorgeous view of Avery bent over the reception desk at Dark Ink. Her ass cheeks poked out from the bottom of a barely-there jean skirt. The woman he had been obsessing over had been looking back at the camera as if daring someone to come push that fabric higher.

If he hadn't been leading the escort of a shipment of electronics for the Minetti family, he could have been here in less than thirty minutes. Instead, his nerves had slowly frayed as he waited for backup to come take his place, hoping Hannibal and Ink could stall her. If she wasn't still here, he might do something regrettable. While he was at the wishing for miracles stage of things, he hoped his kinky Brothers hadn't resorted to extreme measures to keep her here.

He needed to know she was all right, but more than that, he didn't want her hurt any more than she already had been. No matter what his subconscious sent into his dreams, he knew the likelihood of them connecting in a more personal way was slim.

Dark Ink, like most tattoo parlors, was busiest in the evening, and almost every station had an artist and customer filling its space. Hannibal was sitting at his station. The big shit-eating grin on his face let Max know she was still here, but something was up. Neither Ink nor his Wildcat were anywhere in sight.

Max tried to rein in his frustration. His obsession with this woman had grown worse in the last few days as he pored over the information Cami had found. The twenty-seven-year-old woman had been on the fast track to becoming a superstar agent within the DEA until she supposedly went dirty just over a year ago.

Fuck, he of all people knew it was easy to lose your way when undercover, but the more he read, the more convinced he was she'd been set up. Max had helped build enough false cases to recognize one when he saw it. Everything was just a little too perfect. All the evidence lining up with the crafted story. Nothing out of place. Real life was messy, and you often had to interpret and make leaps of logic from the evidence. Rarely did you have everything you needed. But then that could be wishful thinking on his part.

Regardless, for his own sanity, he needed to see her. He never left anything unfinished. Not being able to find her had been like an itch under his skin. Once he figured out what to do about Avery, it would settle everything from the mess last year. Deciding if he would help her or not would depend on what she had to say about her situation.

"Where is she?" Years of practice and undercover work meant he could keep his voice calm even when his insides were a mass of emotions and conflicting desires.

"Ink's keeping her busy in the back." Even with his slow drawl, the man sounded insufferably smug.

Max clenched his fists and took a deep breath. "Keeping her busy?"

Hannibal's smirk showed he heard the jealousy hidden behind his calm words. "She came in for a tattoo, figured giving her some ink was a great way to pass the time." He leaned back on his stool. "You'll never guess what she picked."

Max remembered every blank inch of Avery's caramel skin. That she would come in for her first tattoo while on the run seemed far-fetched. What scheme did she have going on? Did she know that the Dark Sons had been involved in her rescue? He crossed his arms, not in the mood for the southern man's games.

"What?"

Hannibal nodded towards his arm. "Your bike."

The information hit him like a punch. The startlingly realistic Harley on his arm had been a collaboration between him and Ink. It was a nod to his new name and his love of motorcycles. He had earned his Mad Max road name the first time his Brothers saw him riding motocross. Doing tricks and avoiding obstacles while on a racing motorcycle was the only time he felt alive. The speed and tight control needed over his bike and body while racing allowed no other thought to enter his mind. It was an occasional few hours where he had the freedom to forget his past and live in the moment.

He wished he had discovered the sport when he was an out-of-control teenager. Instead, his actions had led him to where he had to choose between jail and the Marines. Bootcamp was where Uncle Sam had found him. His moral flexibility and anger made him perfect for what they wanted. Even though they said, '*Once a Marine, always a Marine*', he never claimed membership with those men because they didn't deserve to be associated with what he had done for his country.

He shook off his thoughts. "That some kind of joke?"

"Nah, your Wildcat picked it out all by herself."

They would have matching tattoos. If a girl he was with had ever suggested such a thing, he would have dropped her quickly. However, the idea of his tattoo on this woman ignited a primal pride he kept locked down deep in his soul. He nodded over at Ink's station. "Why aren't they out here?"

The back area was usually reserved for piercings and tattoos in intimate places. Though his Brothers often took women back there for more carnal pleasures as well. The idea of his fiery Latin wildcat getting intimate with Ink raised his blood pressure.

"Ink thought you might want privacy for your reunion and questioning." He nodded at the curtain that separated the private booths. "They should be almost done. Why don't you let him know you're here."

Max ignored the teasing tone in his Brother's voice and strode to the back. Though he wasn't sure exactly how he was going to handle things, their reunion was long overdue.

The sight that hit him when he stepped past the curtain had his dick jumping to attention. Avery lay sprawled on her side, her gorgeous ass on display barely covered by red satin bikini panties. Her now chestnut hair pooled behind her on the leather chair. Ink was leaned over her hip with a tattoo gun working on what could only be a duplicate of his artwork.

As Max stepped closer, the outline of the road warrior bike looked identical to his. On her curvy body it took on a much sexier appeal. His Brother was a genius with a needle, there was no denying that. Even without shading or color, the piece looked like a photograph captured in her skin.

Ink looked up and smiled. With a slow swipe, he cleared the excess ink and rolled his chair back a bit.

"I think that's enough for today, sweetheart. We can finish up the color next time."

"I can take more." Her voice held a light, flirting tone that seemed off for the powerful woman he remembered.

"I'm sure you can. But I have a surprise for you." Ink nodded over at Max.

Her puzzled expression as she rolled and looked over her shoulder was amusing. Max watched as interest, but surprisingly no recognition, replaced confusion. Since she was here getting his tattoo, he had assumed she had somehow identified him and his Brothers as the ones who had raided the warehouse that day. He tried to keep his own face neutral as he soaked in every sexy detail of her body.

She raised an eyebrow and gave him a smile that was probably supposed to be seductive, but the heat never reached her eyes. "You're my surprise? Not sure what I did to deserve such a generous offering but I'll make sure to do it again." Her voice had dropped into husky tones. She shook her head and looked down, as if embarrassed.

Ink barked a laugh. "Cat, this is my Brother, Max. The man with the tattoo you loved so much."

Max watched carefully as her face went through subtle transitions. An untrained person would have missed the slight widening of her eyes, her lips parting and muscles tightening in fight-or-flight response. She was excited and scared, but covering it well.

Avery sat up. Her body leaned forward in a deliberate motion that gave him a magnificent view down her shirt. "Can I see it?"

Max was suspicious and intrigued by this woman. What a

contradictory mix of personality. It was like he kept getting peeks of the real woman under the fake seductive persona she was trying to display. Pretending to be taken in by her charms, he smiled.

"Sure."

He stepped forward, pushing up the sleeve of his black Henley. When his arm was next to her thigh, he moved it so the tattoos were right next to each other. Ink had mirrored the image so they weren't exactly identical. It was appropriate in a very philosophical way. Both had been undercover agents betrayed by a system they had believed in. They both used secrets and false identities to cover the warriors under their skins.

How had she ended up here? Why had she sought them out? There had to be a plan. Max found himself wanting to play along with her game and discover what she really wanted. Until he figured it out, he could pretend they were strangers. Hopefully, his Brothers would feel the same. The brush of her fingers as they traced over his tattoo broke him from his thoughts.

The small, wistful smile on her face confused him. He knew the look of someone recalling a memory. How had she seen his tattoo back at the warehouse? Their combat gear covered everything. Had she caught a glance while they were wrestling on the ground? His cock punched at his zipper, at the memory of her fire and determination.

Ink leaned in to tape a cotton pad over her tattoo, butting into their private moment. Max traced his fingertips over her knee as he caught her gaze and smirked. "There is a party at the Clubhouse tonight do you want to join me?" Her face tightened in suspicion. Afraid she might not come, he gave her a push. "If you think you can handle it. It gets pretty wild."

He was baiting her. Pricking her ego was the most likely way to get him the desired outcome. He wanted to get her to the Dark Sons compound. Away from any public that might interfere if things got heated. It would be fascinating to see how far she would go to get whatever she wanted. Both Ink and Avery gave him a raised eyebrow. Max knew she would come with him when her lips thinned, followed by a very fake smile.

"Oh, I can handle anything you can."

"I'm sure you can." Max nodded to the hallway. "Bathroom's the last door on the right. It's a half-hour ride."

She snorted. "Yes, Dad. Should I wash my hands and eat my vegetables too?"

He leaned in and caught her gaze. "You always snap at people trying to be nice?"

He could almost feel her struggle not only against him but against herself. Her instincts would be to push back and fight him, but whatever game she was playing required her to play nicely. Her eyes dropped. It was hard to hide his grin as her body language announced she had decided to play along. Her small submission wasn't as exciting as true surrender, but for now it would do.

"I'll be right back." She swung her legs off and stood, taking a moment to straighten her skirt before walking in the direction he had indicated.

Max wanted to chuckle at the tight muscles in her legs that twitched as she walked. The involuntary movements projected loudly how much she didn't want to be doing what he asked.

"What are you up to?" Ink pulled off his latex gloves.

Max made sure Avery was out of earshot before answering. "That woman has ulterior motives and I want to know what they are."

"I thought the point was to help her like you did the other women. Has that changed?"

"No. I'm going to help her but I'm going to do this my way."

The challenge of finding out all this woman's secrets was going to be fun. It had been too long since he had a true interest in a woman. Somehow he knew her trust wouldn't be easy to earn. But the prize would be worth any effort.

Ink chuckled. "I don't think I've ever seen that look on your face, Brother. This is going to be interesting."

Max shrugged. A plan formed in his mind. Trapping his Wildcat was going to be fun.

"Here is what I need you to do."

Chapter 7

Tell me not to do something and I'll do it twice and take pictures.

W hat the hell was she doing? Somehow, in the last few hours, Avery was convinced she had lost all her common sense. Yes, she wasn't a DEA agent anymore, with backup, rules, regulations, or any of the things that came along with that job, but that didn't mean she should throw basic precautions out the window.

Getting on the back of a motorcycle to go to a location she didn't know was just stupid. It was like this man had a straight link to all of her reckless impulses. One moment he had her captivated with his gorgeous eyes and hotter than sin looks, the next she was ready to strangle him for challenging her in such odd ways. The half-hour ride on the back of Max's bike with her arms wrapped around his well-defined stomach had been exhilarating. The thing was like a giant vibrator between her legs, ratcheting up her sexual tension and erasing logical thoughts.

The Clubhouse, and what a joke that name was, took up a huge parcel of land and was more a fortified compound. Four large buildings were visible from the parking lot. The two-story building they went into was bigger than any club in the city. She could pick out a large bar, pool tables, dance floor, tables, and couches scattered throughout the room. Several doors and hallways led out from the main room, meaning there were more areas available than this giant space. With the fifty or so people in the room, the place didn't even feel crowded.

How many men were in this Club that not only could they afford something like this but needed it regularly? She had wondered if she would fit in or stick out with the women who would be here, but shouldn't have worried. The majority of the women scattered through the room were dressed either like strippers or rocker girls. Her short-skirt, tight shirt, and way too high heels fit right in.

"You seem tense." Max sat on a stool at the bar, pulling her in-between his legs with a gentle tug on her belt loops.

The man needed to stop being so sexy. Maintaining a cover had never been difficult for her. In the past there had been handsome men, even a few charming ones whom she had to interact with. Remembering that this was an act shouldn't be hard. Fake flirt, find where they might store the files they took, both physical and digital, and get the hell out. Actual attraction had no place in her plan.

Avery fingered the digital cracker in her pocket she had grabbed from her car before getting swept away on the motor-cycle. She had paid an exorbitant amount of money for the device. The small USB drive would connect with any Windows machine and clone the drive for her to look over later. She had tried it out a few times, and so far it had worked like a charm. If she managed to get alone time with any of their computers tonight, she would be prepared. She forced herself to focus.

"Not tense. Just taking it all in." And trying to figure out why this group of men had rescued her. Attacking that compound, killing all those men, and saving all the women wasn't something that she would have believed an MC known mostly for running guns and protection would be interested in.

"You need to relax. I'm getting us shots." He nodded at the man behind the bar who was wearing a cut with the name Decaf on the shoulder.

"What can I get you, Max?" It was surprising how good looking every one of the men in the black leather cuts was. Did they have some sort of requirement that their members worked out eight hours a day?

"Tequila, line them up."

Avery raised her eyebrow, about to protest. His smirk froze the words in her throat.

"I thought you wanted to have fun, Cat. Was I wrong?"

She barely bit back the growl his challenge deserved. When the first shot was placed on the bar next to them, she gave him a smile that was more a baring of teeth. "You weren't wrong."

She threw back the shot, and while the burn of alcohol slid down her throat, she decided to get a little payback for all the teasing he had been doing. She reached up and grabbed the back of his neck and stepped up onto the first rung of his stool. With her head now above his, she lowered her face until their lips met.

The kiss was a declaration she wouldn't be toyed with. His lips parted, and she took the lead, dancing her tongue with his. He was a good kisser. Nothing extraordinary. Disappointment was a leaden weight in her stomach. After so many sparks, she had hoped for something more.

Seducing him and keeping him on the hook till she got what she needed wasn't going to be a hardship, but it would not be the wild ride she had hoped for either. She stepped down, breaking the kiss. His cock was visibly hard and his eyes held the fire she had hoped would be in the kiss. She had won the challenge he had thrown down, but it was unsatisfying.

"My turn." He moved so quickly she didn't even register it, turning her back to the bar until he had her pinned with his body against its edge.

He leaned forward, his thigh sliding between hers. His chest pressed against hers, the leather of his cut cool against the exposed skin of her stomach. Max's blue eyes captured hers as he slowly swallowed a shot. The sound of the glass hitting the wood barely registered before she felt her head tipped backward by a rough grip in her hair.

All sound faded away except the pounding of her heart in her ears. He didn't kiss her. He claimed her with every part of his body. This was the heat she had wanted. A kiss she would never forget.

Sharp nips to her lips, the rough denim of his pants between her legs, all of it building a sensation that was new and wonderful. She couldn't move if she wanted to, his hands, body and the bar pinning her in place. She wanted the kiss to last forever.

The heat between them flared, and she wanted to crawl inside him. She gripped his shirt. A moan vibrated in her throat as she rubbed against his leg to get the friction she needed. She had never orgasmed from a kiss, but he was starting to make her think it might be possible.

"Oh, I do hate to be a bucket of ice water." A sweet southern twang cut through her haze. "Hawk wants to talk to you, Max."

Max's grip on her hair loosened, and she couldn't help the small sound that escaped her throat. She was torn. Glad they had been interrupted before she completely lost herself in the man she was supposed to be using to get information. Also pissed he stopped before she was ready.

She swallowed, trying to force her pulse and breath back into a normal rhythm. She looked up and was glad to see her own frustration mirrored in Max's face. "Who's Hawk?"

"He's the President."

He said the position like it held weight. Men in the Cartel used titles like that, as if everyone should be ready to bow down and scrape for the people in question. As if being in the leadership of a criminal organization was impressive.

"I guess you better run along quick, then."

His body pushed up against hers. Max's growl against her ear sending chills down her arms.

"I like your spunk, Cat, but don't let it slide into disrespect. You won't enjoy the consequences." He stepped back so quickly she swayed. "You mind keeping Cat company, Val?"

"Sure thing, Sugar. I'll introduce her to the other Old Ladies."

Max nodded and walked away without another word. In his place was a very pregnant redhead. She had big red hair and a glittery t-shirt that read: *The bump gets what the bump wants*. Avery had to smile. The woman named Val was a cross between Reba McEntire and Dolly Parton. She looked familiar.

Avery stumbled a step as she realized how she knew this woman. Last week she had broken into the house of an FBI agent named Victor Taylor. He was the man who had been assigned to coordinate with the DEA on the Recluse case. It had been a desperate act to try to find out who had betrayed her.

After going through his place, Avery was sure he was the

one. Nothing she could present as evidence, but enough oddities to make him suspect number one. This woman's picture had been attached to one of the files she had stolen from his computer. The man had a directory labeled S.T. In it were twenty dossiers. Mostly women and children who lived in the Denver area. The people listed had had no connection she could find with her limited resources.

From what Avery could remember, the file had said this woman was a nurse at a local VA rehab center. Why would an FBI agent have a file on a pregnant nurse?

"So you're Max's woman?" Val's smile was open and inviting, pulling Avery out of her dark thoughts like sunshine on a summer day. She tried to return the smile, doing her best to hide her concern. This was something to worry about later.

"Oh no. We just met," she said as much for her own benefit as Val's. The chemistry between them might be so hot it had almost set her panties on fire, but they were strangers. This was a temporary thing and couldn't last. Even if she didn't go back to the DEA after she cleared her name, he wouldn't want to be with someone who used him to get close to his Club.

Val laughed, and Avery thought it sounded like bells. "You keep thinking that. Come on, the other girls are at a table."

She followed the woman across the room, not sure what else to do. "No, seriously."

"Honey, if you were just another piece of ass, he wouldn't go to all this trouble. Here we are." Her words were confusing, and she couldn't afford to pretend it might become more.

The women sitting around the table were an odd mix. All wore black leather cuts, but that was the only thing they had in common. On the right, a short, plump Asian woman in jeans and a t-shirt sat next to a gorgeous, tall black woman dressed as if she should be selling crystals and natural remedies. On the other side was a cute blonde in a pink sundress sitting next to a purple-haired girl in an elaborate belly dancing costume. None of them looked like what she would picture when someone said biker chick.

Avery's stomach clenched as each of these women's faces sparked a memory. In Agent Taylor's files there was an entry for every one of them. The man had to be targeting the Dark Sons' women. None of it made sense, but she wasn't one to fight against the reality that lay in front of her.

A cold, selfish part of her realized this information would make things both harder and easier. If she didn't find what she needed, maybe she could offer a trade for the information to clear her name. Guilt rolled in her stomach. Could she live with herself if something happened before she shared? Hell, it wasn't like she could just blurt out the information and appear as anything but a lunatic.

"Ladies, this is Max's new friend, Cat. Cat, this is Anna, Queenie, Pixie, and Cami."

Details from the files raced through her brain none of the names matched those in the files, but the pictures left no doubts. Pixie was a new culinary student with an infant son, Queenie, a yoga instructor who managed a spa, Cami a hacker and Anna a home health aide. Avery struggled not to let her concern for these women show.

The black woman rolled her eyes. "I hate that name Val, and you know it. Call me Tari."

Val sat down and gestured to the seat next to her. "But it's so much fun to tease you. It's the only thing that gets you riled up."

Avery took the offered chair, not sure what to say. She had never had female friends and when she was undercover, the women she interacted with were either sex-workers or addicts. She remembered little more from their files, but nothing she had read made her think they were criminals like their men, well except maybe the hacker.

"Nice to meet you."

"That's not the only thing that gets her riled up, Val," the blonde named Pixie teased.

Cami laughed, making the coins on her odd bikini style top jingle. "Well, while you and I might be willing to put on a sex show to get T-Tari's engine racing, I don't think that is the type of fl-flustered Val was thinking of." Her light stutter would have made Avery think she was nervous, but the woman's serene smile said it was just part of who she was.

Avery looked between the two women, a bit confused. "You two are together? I thought you had to be with a man to be part of the Club?"

The entire table burst into laughter, and she tried to hide her embarrassment at speaking before thinking. She needed to get her game together and stop reacting without a plan.

"Oh, Lord." Val slapped the table. "If you two do that, you'll have Tek and Sharp's heads popping like champagne corks. We have to do that sometime after this baby's born so I can be part of the fun."

The girl called Cami bit her lip. "Matching school girl outfits?"

"You *es loco.*" Tari laughed. "Forgive us, Cat, but if you're going to hang with the Old Ladies you should probably get used to it."

"I don't know," Anna said. "The way Max keeps looking over here I think she'll be with us a while."

The temptation to look around for Max to see what the woman was talking about was strong. He had headed into the back area of the room that held the pool tables. But if she turned she might get a glimpse of the gorgeous man. Avery shook her head both to negate her own thoughts and deny the implied connection. "No. We're just going to have some fun."

"Of course." Cami gave each of the women a look that Avery didn't understand. "Where are you from, Cat?"

"Here and there. Mostly Denver." She didn't want to have to make up lies she would need to remember later. If she had known she would be in this situation, she would have made up and memorized a background to use.

"Really?" Tari asked. "I swear you have a New Jersey or maybe Philadelphia accent."

Avery's jaw almost hit the table and Val laughed. "Tari is an expert at accents and languages."

"I grew up in Jersey." Right near Philly but she had thought she had lost that accent after working with some dialect coaches before going under cover. She could fake a Mexican accent and had learned to speak Spanish a few years ago. Her mother had been from Mexico, but she had died when Avery was young and she had never really connected with her heritage.

"We never really lose the accent we grow up with." Tari shrugged.

"You can do that with anyone?" Avery was impressed.

"Pretty much. Though your man is like a blank slate. I'd say Midwestern but it's more generic than that. Ow!" Tari glared at Cami, who had apparently kicked her under the table. "What was that for?"

"Don't g-gossip." A small eye conversation went on between the women. Avery understood she was the outsider here.

"It's okay." She didn't want to cause issues. "This place is much bigger and nicer than I thought it would be." Maybe if she couldn't get them talking about the men, she could get other information. "What are all the buildings for?"

Val smiled. "My man, Dozer, designed most of the compound." She tilted her head, as if considering. "You would have seen the indoor range on the left when you came in. The apartments for the single Brothers, the Clubhouse and the garage they use during winter to the right. A few of us have houses further back but they aren't visible from the parking lot."

"He designed this building? It's huge." Getting people talking wasn't hard when they were proud of something. She felt a small twinge of guilt at manipulating these nice women, but pushed it down.

"Yes, ma'am. Three levels. Bedrooms upstairs for crashing. This level for everyday things and the basement."

"What's in the basement?"

Pixie nodded to the hallway by the bar. "The workout equipment and sparring area, mostly." The cute woman wrinkled up her nose, obviously not a fan of working out.

"The s-server rooms are down there as w-well as Tek's office." Cami gave her an odd look.

The server room would be where the computers were. She tried not to show any excitement. Her feet throbbed, giving her a perfect change of subject.

"That's cool. Ugh. My feet are killing me. Why do we wear these things?" She scooted her chair back showing the thigh high five-inch heels she was wearing.

"Because they make our asses look great," Anna teased.

"Because they make me normal height," Pixie chimed in.

"So Dragon, can fuck me standing up?" Tari winked at her.

All the women laughed at the last one. Cami studied her shoes. "Size eight?"

Avery nodded, surprised the woman could tell with a glance. The woman pulled a tote bag from the back of her chair.

"I have a pair of gladiator sandals you could wear." After a little digging, the woman pulled out a set of strappy black flats. "You can use the bathroom to get ch-changed if you want. It's just down the hall p-past the offices and b-basement door."

Offices and basement. Her pulse kicked up at the idea that

she might get to poke around a little. If nothing else, she could get a peek at where she would need to break into later.

"Why doesn't she just put them on here or use the bathroom right there?" Anna waved to the wall to her left where a restroom sign hung discreetly on the wall.

"She doesn't seem to want to put a show on and with that skirt she would. I prefer the bathroom by the offices." Val shrugged. "Your choice, sweetie, but most people don't know about the other one so less chance of getting an eyeful of one of the Brothers taking a sweetbutt for a ride."

Avery mentally thanked Val for giving her the perfect excuse for snooping. "Not that I'm a prude but I think I'll take the more private choice." She looked over at Cami, trying to hide her eagerness. "If you're sure you don't mind?"

"Not at all." She handed over the sandals.

Her heart hammered in her ears as she made her way through the crowd. Avery kept her body loose so as to not draw attention. The hallway turned almost immediately after she left the main room.

There were no people back here, and even the music was slightly muffled. Avery took the chance, since she was alone, to try every door. The door near the end on the left was marked restroom, and there were four other doors. The first two were locked, and she didn't have anything with her to pick them. The last door on the right opened into a steep stairwell.

This had to be the entrance to the basement with the server room she desperately hoped would be open. She looked around to be sure she was still alone. Avery slipped off her boots so she wouldn't make noise and stepped down, closing the door quietly behind her.

Chapter 8

You don't always need a complicated plan. Sometimes you just need the balls to try.

"This is a crazy ass plan." Highdive, the Club's Sergeant at Arms, complained as he leaned against the pool table.

Max watched Sharp take his shot sinking the striped ball into the corner pocket. It was hard not to show his impatience. Using the Old Ladies to wave temptation in front of his Wildcat wasn't a perfect plan. It was just one of the many ideas he had for forcing things out into the open faster. A long as she took the bait.

He had only recruited Val and Cami to help, knowing they wouldn't mess things up. The other Old Ladies, while wonderful women, wouldn't have the subtlety or devious nature to pull it off. In a perfect world he wouldn't have needed to involve anyone else but unfortunately life usually required compromise.

"What's our liability if she tries something?" Hawk took a swig of his beer. Max was glad to see the Dark Sons' President didn't appear concerned. The man was always in control and just a little distant, he needed to be. Max respected the fuck out of the man who not only led them but was always making sure the over fifty members of the chapter were doing well.

"Not much." Tek shrugged. "Nothing in her file says she has the computer skills to hack us. She can't be hiding much in that outfit she's wearing, so no threat of a bomb or weapon. Surveillance cameras are recording her movements. Not that it matters right now because she's right there sitting with our women."

Max looked across the large room and saw through the small crowd that Avery was sitting with five of the Old Ladies. They were laughing and having a good time.

"I don't think she's a physical threat or I wouldn't have brought her here," he said.

"Why did you bring her here?" Dozer asked. The Treasurer of the Dark Sons was a large man with a graying beard who right now resembled a pissed off muscular Santa Claus. Getting his pregnant wife involved hadn't originally been part of Max's plan. Cami had insisted on letting her in on it and no one had stopped her.

"She needs help."

"Then you should have helped her like you did the others." Dozer growled and stepped into his space. "Anonymously with our cash and contacts. Not exposed our women to a fucking murderer."

His Brother's anger was like a physical blow that pushed Max's temper to the surface. None of the men or women here were innocents, so the insult to his Wildcat was unnecessary and hypocritical. This plan might have been last minute but he had done everything he could to make this low risk. He took a calming breath and tried to think of a response that would de-escalate the situation.

Dozer's chest bumped his and Max's calm snapped. "Pixie's a fucking murderer and your woman hangs out with her every day." He leaned into Dozer's face. "I didn't ask for your woman to be involved. You know I'd die to keep your Old Lady safe, so how about you cut me and Cat some fucking slack?"

Dozer's body tensed and Max stepped sideways. The punch that would have taken him in the jaw glanced off his shoulder. He didn't want to hurt the man who was worried about his pregnant wife but there was no way he was going to let him get a shot in.

He stepped to the side blocking the next punch. His Brother was lost in his rage. Max avoided the next few blows dodging around the pool table. He slipped sideways after a particularly wild swipe intending to wrap the man up in a hold. Max's breath exploded out of him as a kick to his stomach sent him stumbling back a step.

The pool table scraped against the floor moving as Dozer slammed into it. Max spun ready to fight for real but was brought up short. Hawk stood between them with a fire in his eyes that said he would take no more of their shit. His glower alone was enough to have lesser men pissing their pants. How the fuck had he missed the older man moving between them?

"Dozer, stand down." Hawk turned his gaze on the Treasurer. "There are four brothers within feet of your woman to keep her safe." The President's glare turned on him. "Max find your chill or I'll call this whole thing off and get the info we need the old-fashioned way." The room should have lost at least five degrees with the ice in those words.

"For the record—" Highdive put his pool cue down on the table. "I want it known that you all turn into a bunch of nutbags when complicated pussy comes around. Fuck, it's been too quiet here anyway. Is your woman likely to get kidnapped, Max? Cause that seems to be the new requirement to become an Old Lady."

Max chuckled and tried to breathe out his tension. Hawk's kick had winded him.

"Already saved her from that once so we should be good." Was he admitting he wanted her as an Old Lady? Damn, talk about making wild leaps of thought.

"Fuck, does that mean this is going to be easier or harder?" Highdive shook his head.

"Doesn't matter." Hawk stared at them each in turn, a small smile barely tipping his lips. "Max asked us to do this. I agreed. You saying you're not up to the challenge?"

Highdive held up his hands in surrender. "Just seeing if I should order in some extra ammo."

They all chuckled and, just like that, the angry mood was broken. Max was happy when Dozer gave him a chin lift to show he wasn't still ready to fight. It was good to be reminded that no matter what, they were Brothers and would have each other's backs. They bullshitted for a few minutes until Cami slipped through the crowd and up to the pool tables. She gave each of them a worried look.

"She's headed to the b-bathroom." Her words had them snapping to attention all pretense at relaxing gone.

Max nodded to Hawk. "If she takes the bait I'll confront her downstairs. You guys are backup in the hall if she manages to get by me."

"What if she doesn't take the bait?" Cami's innocent question made him shake his head.

Max thought about it for a second. "Whatever else that woman is, she's desperate. My Wildcat doesn't have enough sense to be afraid. She'll take the bait."

Chapter 9

If you don't want to get burnt, you shouldn't play with fire.

The stairway down to the basement was pitch black. The dim light from the LEDs scattered around the ridiculously large workout area had been a pleasant surprise. These guys had to have enough workout equipment to furnish a professional gym. Beyond the equipment and the large mat, which could hold twenty people easily, had been another small hallway.

Behind one door had been an enormous bathroom with several showers. Past that, a large split closet filled with towels and the last door had been the server room. She should be happy that everything had gone so smoothly, but instead her nerves were tingling like firecrackers.

Racks of servers were against the back wall, humming with power. On a desk was a monitor and computer setup she hoped would interface with everything. Of course it had been password protected, so she had plugged in her device and prayed. Avery stood watching the lights blink, hoping that meant it was doing its job.

Finally, the light went out indicating the download was complete. She slipped the expensive USB into her pocket and took a deep breath. Not knowing what she was looking for or where they would keep it meant she might have nothing of value on the small electronic device.

The opportunity had just been too good to pass up. She needed any information they had about her from the files they had taken last year. It was a long shot, but she prayed there would be proof of who had actually killed her partner, or at least records that would prove who had blown her cover.

Avery slipped out of the server room as quietly as she could. She needed to get back upstairs before Max noticed she was gone. Hopefully, his *'men only'* conversation would still be going on, and no one would notice her brief side trip. She was about halfway through the workout area when a scraping sound echoed through the room. She spun, ready to face whoever was down here with her.

Max stood, his hands braced above him on a pull-up bar. His face a cold, blank mask. Fuck. She would have to brazen this out and hope he bought it.

"Hey, Max. Your meeting done?" She put a sway into her step and closed the distance between them until she pressed against his chest. When her hands met his chest, that strange electricity jumped between them again. Guilt pricked at her heart. This gorgeous man didn't deserve her lies, but what choice did she have?

If she didn't clear her name, her life was all but over. The fantasy of finding out if the chemistry between them could blossom into something bigger was impossible. She slipped her hands under his shirt, enjoying the feel of his muscles against her fingers. Maybe she could give in to the heat and give them what they both wanted. Plus, maybe he would get distracted and not question her about why she was down here.

He stepped back from her, pulling off his cut and placing it folded onto the weight bench. Avery bit her lip as he pulled off his Henley, enjoying the sight of his beautifully tattooed chest. Next, he pulled out a gun from a holster behind his back and placed it on the bench next to his clothes. He toed off his boots and socks. Damn, a man's feet shouldn't be sexy but his were.

He stalked forward, his eyes lit with a feral danger. She couldn't help but retreat backwards onto the mat that took up most of the floor. Her own aggression rose to meet his. A primal growl, almost animalistic, echoed in the quiet room. The sound appealed to some dark part of her psyche.

Max stepped onto the soft surface and shook his head. "You are playing with fire. I'd say run but then I'd just hunt you to ground."

"We fighting or fucking?" Teasing him was such a bad idea, but it was like he was a challenge she couldn't back down from.

"That's the point, Wildcat. I want to do both."

Avery froze at the nickname he had used for her over a year ago, fear chilling the aggression that had pumped through her system. Then rage boiled up from her stomach. "You know who I am, don't you?"

"From the moment you stepped into the shop." Max's wink was so condescending she gave an angry growl of her own.

Those assholes. They had been playing with her all along. Her anger and adrenaline mixed into an explosive wave of emotion. She charged at him, a scream ripping out of her throat. He dodged her kick. The sensation of her fist hitting the solid wall of muscle that was his abs made her bare her teeth in a smile as she ducked under his arm. He tried to grapple her and she spun away out of his arms.

They circled each other, crouched low. Never once did it occur to her to run. She needed this. Needed to be able to fight and let out the anger and frustration that had been building inside of her. She did a low leg sweep, trying to knock him down, but he got a grip on her ankle and pulled her off balance.

Avery's back hit the soft mat with a breath stealing thud and she found herself face to face with Max. His expression was a mixture of need and joy that should have been impossible, but she completely understood. This was real. No fake trappings of civilization, just two animals battling for dominance. She lifted her head and nipped his lip.

The kiss he answered with was an exquisite claiming, brutal and wild. She clawed at his back as if trying to climb inside him. He held her hair in a rough grip, moving her head how he wanted as he explored every inch of her mouth. When they broke apart, their breath was coming in loud pants.

"Why were you down here, Wildcat?"

Fuck, how could he be asking that question now? Her brain was working on a one word basis. Mine. More. Now. Want. She tried to focus and remember her mission. It didn't change if they knew who she was.

"Curiosity."

He bit down on the juncture where her neck met shoulder and her body spasmed in both pain and pleasure. "And what were you doing in the server room?"

"Nothing." She gasped as his tongue licked along the bruise he had caused.

He sat up and gripped the front of her shirt in both hands. The pull and tear as he managed to not only rip apart her shirt, but her bra also, had gooseflesh rolling over her skin in excitement. It didn't matter if he believed her, as long as he didn't stop what he was doing.

He bit down on her collarbone, then her breasts. The marks he left behind on her dusky skin would last for days and she would love looking at them, reliving this moment over and over. Never before had she enjoyed herself so perfectly. Her past lovers had been tame, their idea of rough sex a cute slap to her ass upon request. She needed this, needed him.

Lightning sparks of pleasure and pain forced a scream out of her as he bit each nipple leaving them wonderfully throbbing and aching for more. The world spun for a moment and before she understood what he was doing, he had her kneeling up and facing away from him. His powerful arms pinned her arms to her side as they wrapped above and below her breast, trapping her back to his chest. Strong legs pressed against her thighs as he knelt behind her immobilizing her legs as well.

Max bit her ear. The pain helped bring her mind back into focus. "What were you doing in the server room?"

It was obvious he knew something, and it was tempting to confess everything. It had been so long since anyone had been on her side the urge to share her problems was like a giant lump sitting in her stomach. But she couldn't. Trusting people was how she got into this mess. Believing in the system that claimed to take care of their own. How fast had their belief in her gone when she had been accused of being dirty?

Not one person had believed her story. Not one person had fought on her side or even doubted for one moment that she was guilty. Co-workers and friends all stopped answering her calls. Gave her dirty looks at the pre-trial hearings. She was alone in the world, and it was better that way.

She snarled. "I was just looking around."

Avery threw her weight to the side and pulled her knees up, trying to get some leverage. The frustrating man's only reaction was to hold her tighter, constricting her breath. His hand slid down, she thought to steady her hips. Too late, she realized he was slipping his hand into the pocket of her skirt that held the USB drive.

She bucked, but it was useless. The sight of him snapping the device in half between his fingers enraged her. With a scream she ducked her chin and bit down on the arm pinning her chest in place. His snarl made her laugh, and he pulled her head back by her hair with the hand that no longer held her precious data.

"Biting me only turns me on more, Wildcat. Now tell me why you tried to hack our computers."

She felt her own excitement starting to drip down her thighs. This whole encounter was messed up on a level she couldn't even start to break down. He was the enemy, so she should not want him to use the large cock she felt pressing against her ass to fuck her until she passed out. She could blame it on the fantasies of the last year, but the truth was she had always been wired slightly off normal.

Where other women dreamed of sweet men who cuddled and talked about their feelings, she had wanted someone to match her strength and fire. What was the point in choosing a partner who was weaker than herself? Every man she had dated in the past, even if they had been willing to be in charge, had wanted her to make herself something lesser rather than stepping up their game and being something better.

Max had out thought her, out fought her and at no point had he tried to make her be less. He seemed to revel in her strength. Could she trust him with even a small portion of her secrets? Would he help her? If he did, would he really help or just try to sideline her while he tried to take over?

Out of options, she felt a small part of the wall around her heart crumble. Telling him the truth was a wild chance, but what did she have to lose? "I need the information you stole from Mitchell Thomas to prove I didn't kill my partner."

The arm around her chest loosened and she felt light brushes over her sensitive nipples. She couldn't look down to see what he was doing because of his grip on her hair and that made the sensations more intense. He circled one then the other, the touches getting firmer and she could feel her heartbeat in each nipple as they tightened painfully, aching for a stronger touch.

"What do you think is in that information?"

She paused, not wanting to admit she wasn't sure what she wanted to find. His rough palm slid down her stomach and pulled her skirt. It caught for a second on the bandage covering her tattoo, then slid the rest of the way up so her soaked panties would be fully exposed. Her arms were free now and she could have fought him, but she didn't want to. What she wanted was for him to slip his hand inside her underwear and ease the ache that was now a pulsing pain centered around her core.

"Mitchell found out I was an undercover Federal Agent. He and that bastard Mateo set me up for the murder and to be kidnapped and raped. The job they did wasn't some quick scam. I hope there is something. Maybe the woman they used to pose as me, maybe the real source of the fake account found in my name. Anything at this point would be useful." Her last word was gasped as he finally slid his fingers down through her slit.

His light touch was perfect and maddening. He swirled around her clit and heat built as her pussy clenched wanting something inside her. She squirmed, trying to get the friction she needed to push her closer to climax.

"Why didn't you just ask for our help?" His fingers slid down just sliding inside her entrance.

She laughed, her breath hitching as he started fucking her

with his fingers at a frustratingly slow pace. "Why would a bunch of criminals want to help me?"

"Pot." He nipped her neck. "Kettle." He bit down hard on her neck, the ache shooting down her spine.

Her mind raced as she realized just how stupid her words were. He was right. She was judging them without knowing them, like so many others judged her. Hell, she really was a criminal now. Breaking in and stealing files from both the District Attorney and the FBI agent had required the commission of several crimes. She had killed the two women in jail. It had been self-defense, but that didn't make it any less of a sin. She moaned as he began pushing deeper inside her, his grip on her neck and hair keeping her pinned and at his mercy.

His complete control over her body let her mind float, and she felt all the emotions of the last year washing over her in waves. She hated being alone without backup. Working for the DEA had given her, if not a family than a safety system. She hadn't realized how much she missed that until now. She leaned into Max's body, enjoying for just this moment not having to do anything but feel what he was doing to her body.

His grip loosened, and she felt his tongue do a gentle sweep up her neck. "You're going to let me help you."

She jerked as his two talented fingers found her G-spot and began stroking against it. An orgasm like she had never felt started building deep inside her. "You'll give me the information?"

He nipped her earlobe. "If we have it. But I'm going to help you clear your name."

"Why would you do that?" The crazy things he was doing to her body weren't making it easy to concentrate. She needed to understand what he was offering.

"Because you're mine."

The words made no sense, but she felt them deep in her bones. Pleasure built like an ache along her spine. Logic and reality were inconsequential. She needed to come, and she needed him to make the stress of the last year disappear.

"If I'm yours, why aren't you fucking me?"

His growl vibrated down her spine as he pushed her down onto all fours.

"Be good, Wildcat." His breath was warm against her back. "Or I'll leave you hot and wanting. Only good girls get to come."

She bucked against him, frustrated at how easily he held her pinned.

"Of course, I owe you a punishment for coming down here so your choice. No orgasm or you stay on your knees like the naughty girl you are and let me spank you."

She tossed her head, throwing her hair over her shoulder so she could glare at him.

"Can't you multi-task? If you want me to let you spank me, you better be fucking me at the same time." She wanted to feel him inside her, not play some stupid game. Most men would give up on playing games when sex was on the table. Avery wasn't sure if she hoped Max would be like all the rest, or if for once she would find a man who would live up to his promises.

Chapter 10

I haven't lost all my marbles yet, but there's a small hole in the bag somewhere.

Max loved her fire. The way she challenged him even from her knees had his cock so hard it pushed painfully against his jeans. Claiming her as his wasn't logical, but it was real. He reached around the front of her, undoing the button of her jean skirt. With a yank he pulled both it and her panties down to her thighs, using the material to hobble her.

She bucked, and he caught her arms behind her back. Her snarl was exciting as hell as he eased her forward and pinned her face down on the mat. He wanted her like he had never desired a woman before. But he had to be sure she wanted this too.

"I'm going to spank your ass till it's cherry red, then fuck you till you're seeing stars. You don't want this, you say stop.

But no other word is going to make one difference in the outcome."

"Fuck you!" She tried to twist out of his grip, but he kept her pinned. Her struggles only revved up his desire. She was perfect in this moment, wild and raw. Her fight, her desire, the unique blaze that was her soul was everything he could want in that moment. All that was left was for him to earn her submission.

His hand came down on her ass with a satisfying crack. "Those definitely weren't the right words."

Time lost meaning as he spanked her. She twisted and cursed, but never once asked him to stop. He could feel the anger and pain that she was finally able to release through her screams. Tears, he somehow knew she never let herself shed, slid down her cheeks as she gave it all over to him. Max knew what she needed. The physical pain allowed her an outlet for the emotions she kept bottled inside.

He was careful to spread out the blows, pushing her body's responses higher. When she started arching up into his blows rather than trying to avoid them, he knew it was time. Her ass and upper thighs were a beautiful deep red that meant she was going to remember his touch for days. He had avoided the taped off area around her tattoo, not wanting to damage the beautiful artwork that connected them.

Holding her down with one hand, he slipped off his jeans. She panted against the mat lost in the high of the endorphins from his spanking. He wrestled her skirt and panties off her legs, loving the pool of her cream below her pussy that showed she was enjoying this as much as he was. He lifted his hand, running a light touch down her spine. There it was. True submission. She held still for him without a fight, wanting what only he could give her.

A possessive urge filled his chest with a heat that shot straight to his cock. He needed to claim her and mark her in the most basic of ways. He leaned down to her ear and with his last ounce of self-control whispered, "Do I need a condom, Wildcat? I'm clean and want to fuck you raw."

Her breath slowed for a minute, then caught as she processed his words. "I'm on birth control. I have an IUD and I'm clean. Hasn't been a lot of opportunity to fool around while trying to stay alive."

"Is that a yes?"

"Yes." The word was as much a demand as consent.

He bit her earlobe, growling in satisfaction. "Then run."

He gave her ass one last smack and loved the way she sprang up into a sprint. She was beautiful and someday he would enjoy truly chasing her, but tonight wouldn't be that time. He couldn't wait. Max tackled her before she got five steps and rolled with her on the padded floor. The minx managed to wrap her legs around him and as they tumbled. The feel of her wet pussy over his length was a temptation. The pleasure that shot through him was distracting and she somehow ended up on top of him.

He arched back and then pushed his hips forward to slide into her hot depths. He gripped her hips and thrust up into her, not letting her take control. She moaned in time with his motions, and he felt her constrict around him. Her nails against his chest were sharp pricks that drove his passion higher. She clawed at him. He was sure she was unaware of the damage she was doing so lost in the sensations of their joining. Her hips bucked against him, and her raw scream filled the room as her orgasm clutched at his cock.

He took a minute to enjoy the tight grip of her pussy spasming around him before he rolled them so she was pinned underneath him. This was where they belonged. Locked together in the most primal dance between two people.

He pulled back and slammed into her depths, finally releasing his own control. His deep growls and her screams echoed off the walls. They weren't people anymore, they were animals caught in the most basic of drives. Perfectly in sync with the natural rhythm of their bodies. Male claiming female. The strength of his body matching the fire of her soul to become something more than just individuals.

Max's orgasm started deep in his spine, but he was determined to see her break apart for him one more time. His Wildcat clawed at his arms and back like the wild woman she was. Each little hurt fueled his pleasure. He ground them together and bit the wonderful spot right at the side of the base of her throat.

Her pussy gripped him in waves, and her screams turned to gasping moans. Only then did he let himself go. The pleasure was like a white supernova passing through his body. His arms trembled, ready to collapse, so he rolled them. Pliant and spent, she cuddled perfectly against his chest. Their breaths and hearts slowed as they both basked in the moment.

A slow clapping filled the room, and Max looked up to see Hawk and the other officers at the edge of the sparring mat. Amused smiles on their faces.

Hawk tossed a few towels in their direction. "Clean up. Bring her to my office. We need to talk."

Chapter 11

When you've hit rock bottom there is only one way to go.

S he had lost her mind. That was the only explanation for what had happened in the basement. Now she was being led like a prisoner up the stairs and to a meeting with a stranger. At least Max had given her his shirt to wear, but his distracting leather and pine scent was now wrapped all around her.

It was tempting to try to run when they reached the hall-way, but the two large men from the tattoo shop, Hannibal and Ink, blocked her path out of the Clubhouse. What the hell would these guys have to say to her? She didn't believe for one minute they would want to help her. Men said a lot of things they didn't mean when they wanted sex. Now that she and Max had fucked like rabid bunnies with an audience, all his big words would be worthless.

They walked into a nice but overly masculine office. The man who had demanded their presence sat behind a gorgeous oak desk. Pictures and memorabilia of all things military and motorcycle covered the walls. Several comfy looking chairs were arranged in front of the desk and scattered around the room. Behind the man in charge, who's cut read Hawk, was an overly muscled man with a patch that said Sharp. The door thudded intimidatingly as Max shut it, locking the four of them alone in the small space.

Sharp's smile was teasing as he looked at Max. "You going to need stitches?"

Avery felt her cheeks heat. Since Max was shirtless because of her, it was easy to see the red marks she had left on his chest and arms. He had put on his cut, but it covered little of the damage. To her embarrassment, a few of them were seeping blood. Memories of lashing out at him a few times were vivid in her mind, but she did not remember turning him into a scratching post.

"I think I'll survive." Max nodded to the chair in front of him like he expected her to sit in it.

It was tempting to refuse, but honestly she was exhausted. The energetic and mind blowing orgasms had been a release of so much more than sexual tension. She felt like she had gone through both a physical and emotional obstacle course and was trying not to collapse on the finish line. Most people got to snuggle and fall asleep after sex. Instead she was about to be questioned and God knew what else.

She flopped into the chair. Pain made her wince as her bruised ass thumped onto the chair. Her whole body was covered in bruises from his bites. She hated and loved each mark.

Sitting there barefoot, covered in the evidence of his dominance, put her off kilter. She should have taken the time to put on her boots. Clothes were her armor, and she needed as much as she could get right now.

Hawk flipped open a folder in front of him. "Avery Perez.

Born in Camden, New Jersey. Entered the foster care system at age eight. Graduated in three years from Rutgers with a degree in Criminal Justice. Hired by the Drug Enforcement Agency, graduated training with honors. Worked undercover for four years the last two as a money launderer for the Cartels." He looked up and held her gaze. "Accused of murdering her partner Nathan Chatham and taking bribes to give confidential information to those same cartels. You killed two women while in jail and managed to escape during transport with the help of unnamed accomplices. And now you're a bad thief." He flipped the folder shut.

Avery shook her head, pissed at his obvious taunting. She knew what the file probably contained. She had stolen a file exactly like it from the prosecutor's house. Like a life could be broken down into only a few pages. Most of the information was bullshit after she entered the DEA. Avery wasn't sure if that was because of the classified nature of her work or part of the bigger frame job. Yeah, she had been undercover, but the things listed weren't even close to the truth that had been her life.

"What do you want me to say?"

"Who helped you escape?" Hawk's gaze was intense. He might have graying hair, but nothing about him was old or weak. If she was anyone else, he might be intimidating, but when you have faced drug lords and psychopaths his hard stare was only mildly impressive.

"Why do you care?"

Sharp leaned forward on the desk, and Max took a step closer to her. It was hard to read their body language, but it seemed like Sharp was threatening her and Max was stepping in to defend her, but that couldn't be right.

"Answer his question," Sharp growled. His deep voice had nothing on Max's.

She raised an eyebrow. "I know you all think you are scary

with the muscles and leather you got going on, but seriously, if I didn't answer questions when being threatened with rape and beatings I'm not going to be intimidated by stern voices and big muscles."

"Behave, Wildcat. We're trying to help you." Max's voice sounded exasperated.

It was so tempting to trust him. She was near the end of her rope with no other leads other than these men and the files from the FBI agent that she didn't understand. She had considered trying to kidnap Agent Taylor but no matter how many laws she had broken in the last month, she didn't think torturing a man to get answers was something even the new her could do.

"No one helped me escape."

Sharp snorted. "You escaped two trained guards while shackled in the rear of a van. I saw your moves downstairs and they are impressive but not enough to overcome weapons and restraints."

Her laugh held no humor. "I didn't escape from the back of a van. I escaped from a shack in the woods while one of them was undressing to rape me and the other was transferring my shackles to a rusty bed frame." The memory of what happened in that dirty room that smelled of mold and animal shit tried to rise up. She clenched her fists and pushed it down.

"They were raping you?" Max's anger was like a hot wave while Hawk's and Sharp's gazes had gone cold.

At least these men had enough of a soul to not condone rape. The world was filling up with shades of gray the more she looked around. All criminals weren't evil and all law men weren't good. It had been the hardest part of her time in jail. Letting go of the ignorant belief in pure good and evil.

"Trying. I disabled them both and escaped." She gritted her teeth as a wave of nausea turned her stomach. "Wasn't sure if Jones was going to survive after I shot him with his own gun. Didn't much care as his pants were undone and he had said he was going to tear me up before he killed me."

"What the fuck?" Sharp pushed back and paced a few steps behind his president.

Hawk studied her like searching for a hidden meaning in her words. She was used to people not believing her, and was ready for these men to be the same. She was surprised when he settled back into his chair and asked, "Did they tell you why they attacked you?"

"Other than the obvious part of them being assholes?" She shook her head. "Yeah, the money on my head had gotten too tempting to pass up. But if they were going to kill me anyway, they might as well have fun first."

"Fuck." Max's curse said it all.

The price on her head had steadily increased every month she was in jail. It had reached ten thousand dollars the first time she had learned of it. Her cell mate, desperate for drug money, had jumped her in the shower with an improvised shiv. The guard who was supposed to be watching her had been conveniently distracted. Over the next few months the amount had grown and when the guards attacked her, they claimed it was a hundred thousand dollars. The people funding that money was up for speculation, but she guessed it was the cartel. Mateo had been a big player in Denver with family members higher up in the cartel. If they blamed her for his death, they would probably not stop until they killed her. Knowing that was hard because that meant even if she managed to clear her name, she would probably always be in danger.

"Yeah, sucks to be me." Avery laughed. "Life is just one big party, right?"

"All right, Cat, you are going to tell us everything and we are going to see what we can do." Hawk's voice held both demand and promise.

Shock hit her like a blow to the chest. "Why?"

Avery looked at the three men in the room dressed in black with biker vests proclaiming them outlaws. She wasn't about to turn down help, but if this came with some hidden price, she wanted to know about it up front. "No offense, but why would a bunch of gun-running criminals be interested in helping out an ex-DEA agent who is wanted by the law?"

She did have information they needed, but there was no way they knew that. She paid her debts. Regardless if these men helped or not, she would give them the files on their women. If something bad happened to those funny crazy girls, she would never forgive herself.

Sharp looked offended, but Hawk steepled his fingers in front of his face. "What have you heard about the Dark Sons?"

"You run guns and a protection racket. You have connections to lots of other criminal organizations. Since you don't ever get involved with drugs, you weren't anything but a footnote in DEA files I read."

Hawk nodded and leaned back. "Every man in this chapter, every member of the Dark Sons nationally, has one thing in common outside our Patch. It is the only thing that can't be ignored or overlooked when you want to be one of us. We, all of us, have served at least three years in service to our country or a cause bigger than the individual. Some have done that in the usual manner by serving overseas in the military," he nodded to Sharp, "others have gone less traditional routes." His gaze flicked to Max. "What that means is every one of us knows what it means to put the needs of a larger purpose over our own desires. Even if doing so ended in betrayal or abandonment once our time was up. The Dark Sons are loyal to our own. Max wants to help you, so we will all help you no matter what you think of who we are."

His words were a slap in the face. She had been judging

them without all the information. Running guns was wrong, but that didn't mean the people who did it were inherently evil. Hell, how many times had she seen operations in her own organization that looked evil from the outside. It was nice to believe that what they did served a greater good, but often the bad guys got away with it and the agents had broken the law for nothing.

"I apologize." The words were bitter on her tongue, even if she meant them. "It is hard to trust when so many have turned on you."

"You going to let us take care of this for you?" Max's question fired back up all the anger she had released.

"No, but if you want to help me clear my name I am willing to take that help." There was no way she was being cut out of this. She needed to be part of everything to regain control of her own life. She wouldn't hand everything over and sit back trusting they would take care of things for her.

"It's not safe," Max growled, waking up urges she had thought had been fully satisfied. "You are on the most wanted list with the cops. You need to go into hiding. We'll handle this."

The patronizing meaning behind his words was like a match to her anger. "I'm not going to sit back. This is *my* life. You cavemen might think women are only good for one thing, but fuck that. I help or I'm gone."

Max stepped closer, and she jumped to her feet, not willing to let him loom over her in some macho attempt at intimidation. "Where are you going to go, Wildcat? Back to that shitty hotel with the cash under the mattress and a pathetic arsenal of weapons?"

How the fuck had they found her hotel? Her bruises throbbed as her muscles clenched, ready for a fight. Her car. They must have found something to lead them back to her room. While she had been here, they must have been busy boys. "Don't you worry about me. I can take care of myself. Think I'm impressed that you can break into a twenty-year-old car and find one of my safe-houses? I think you should be worried more about your own women." She leaned in, getting up into his face. "The culinary student, yoga instructor, hacker, and nurse are in danger and you don't even know about it."

Max stepped back like she had slapped him. She hadn't meant to let that drop, but it was like Max triggered all her reckless tendencies. There was no point in backing down. She would trade the info she had for the information she needed and forget all about this condescending asshole and his band of leather wearing Brothers. From the angry looks on their faces, they were no longer interested in helping her anyway.

"What the fuck do you know about our women?" Sharp's angry question hung in the air.

Avery took a deep breath, pulling herself back together. She blanked her face. "I know that a very dangerous man is collecting information on them as targets. I have that information and will trade it and the identity of that man for what you have then we go our separate ways." The last part of the sentence hurt because she didn't want to never see Max again, but it was the only logical thing.

Sharp looked ready to come around the desk and strangle her, but Hawk's hand on his arm seemed to hold him in place. She turned to see Max's disappointed expression. Had he been imagining something more between them than the one time? It was silly to think so. The chemistry between them might be off the charts, but that didn't make up for the fact that anything between them was impossible.

"And if we don't have the information you need?" Max's words were cold, but his eyes showed the anger underneath.

Would she hold back the information? No. That wasn't who she was. The adrenaline seemed to flow out of her body.

She slumped with exhaustion, the last of her reserves expended. Why was she bothering with this posturing? She was tired, body and soul. Tomorrow she would find the strength to go on, but not at the expense of innocent women. She sighed. "Fuck it. The information is in a safe behind the back right side panel of my car. Bring my car here and I'll give it to you and get out of your hair. I'll give you a contact number and hope you'll have enough decency to contact me if you find anything."

Hawk's mouth quirked up at the corner. "Put her in lockdown at your place, Max. Talk some sense into her."

Lockdown didn't seem like something she would enjoy. Hell, she knew she wouldn't, but what choice did she have? Maybe after some sleep and some time to soak everything in she would resist, but for now she would play along.

It would save her from having to find a place to sleep until she could get her things back or stocking back up. She may have pretended to have multiple safe-houses, but the truth was the hotel room and her car was it.

Sharp shook his head. "Where did you get the files?"

"Agent Victor Taylor, the asshole I think set me up. The files were on his computer. I didn't know who the people were till I saw them sitting out there." Avery gestured behind her to the main area of the Clubhouse.

"Was it just Pixie, Val, Tari, and Cami in the files?" Max asked.

"No, there were a lot more but I don't know if they all have to do with your Club."

Hawk looked over at Sharp. "Send out an alert until we learn more. Make sure the Brothers keep their Old Ladies tight."

"There were some children in those files too," she couldn't help but add.

"Right. Families too." Sharp strode past them and out the door without another word.

Hawk looked up at her and Max standing in front of him his face tight. "It's a good thing you offered up those files, Cat. I don't take well to blackmail. You aren't family yet and there is only so much I'm willing to take from a Civilian. Get her out of here before I change my mind."

Max grabbed her arm, and she didn't fight him. What the hell did he mean by she wasn't family yet?

"He knows my name isn't Cat, right?"

Max's chuckle wasn't comforting as he escorted her out of the office.

"It is now."

Chapter 12

Home is where your crazy matches the curtains.

Max had brought no one other than his Brothers to his house, so opening the door for the surprisingly compliant woman at his side sent a strange sense of tightness to his stomach. The name Cat suited her. Sleek grace, vicious claws, and a dangerous aura that made you want to get close. She didn't realize how close she had come to finding out how not on the right side of the law his Brothers were. With Old Ladies in danger, they would not have let her walk out of that room without giving up the information.

As a rule his Brothers didn't hurt innocents, but every one of them would throw the rulebook out the window for the safety of family. He didn't want to imagine where that would have placed him. The volatile connection between him and Cat was new and intense. Would he have stepped between her and his Brothers if she had refused to tell? Did it matter? If she was the type of person to use the safety of women for her own means, he hoped it would have killed the attraction between them.

"Wow, you really like bikes."

His house on the Dark Sons compound was the first place he had ever called home. For the last three years he had filled it with things he loved. The walls and shelves were covered with a mix of memorabilia from classic Harleys to his favorite Honda CRF450 that he used in motocross. Several pictures on the walls were gifts from his Brothers, framed pictures of him doing stunts at the charity events they put on like the one that was happening tomorrow.

"I do." He stepped up behind her as she looked up at a picture. It was a great shot that had captured his bike and the sky at an angle that made it look like he was flying. "It's the ultimate mix of freedom and control."

She looked up at him and he wanted nothing more than to take her lips and claim her body again, but they had things to work out. He stepped back and enjoyed the disappointed glare she gave him.

She cleared her throat. "Who is that in the picture?"

"It's me." Max moved to the kitchen and pulled out two beers from the fridge. "You want a drink?"

She followed him and sat on a stool at the breakfast bar. Her wince as her ass hit the chair made him have to hide a grin. "Sure. That's an amazing photo."

They sat in silence for a few awkward minutes, sipping their drinks.

"I'll show you your room."

"I guess we should talk."

They spoke at the same time.

He chuckled. Of course, she wouldn't want to avoid the conversation. His Wildcat was anything but meek.

She stuck out her hand. "Hi, I'm Avery, escaped prisoner trying to clear my name by stealing information from your biker gang." She dropped her hand onto the counter with a huff. "I feel like I'm living a bad made for TV spy movie." Her sigh was filled with exhaustion. "Not sure anyone would believe the plot though."

He placed his hand on hers and gave it a squeeze. "Club, not gang, and yes, life is rarely as clean cut as the movies. The good guys don't always wear the badge and the bad guys don't always have a goatee." He took a sip of his beer and smiled. "Besides, you have a new name now so your new story can start now."

"Is that how it works? New name wipes out the past." Her raised disbelieving eyebrow made him chuckle. "That would be convenient but not practical. I still have a price on my head no matter what anyone calls me."

"Doesn't wipe out the past. I have found that it can let you set yourself on a new path."

She took a pull off her beer and looked away, obviously uncomfortable with the idea. "How come you don't get a cool name like all your Brothers? Was Studly already taken, so you refused to settle on anything else?"

"Brat." The abrupt change of subject was an obvious deflection, but he let her do it. "Max is my road name. Ever see the Mad Max movies? Well after watching me do motocross my Brothers thought it was fitting."

"Ink mentioned that the bike on your tattoo was from there. Guess I didn't put it together." She looked down at where the tattoo was on her own body. "Hope you don't mind me stealing your idea."

"Not at all, but I'm surprised you went through with it."

"Why? Did you think a little pain would be a deterrent to me?" Her smile was more of a baring of teeth.

"Put your claws away, Wildcat." He paused and waited

until she took a long breath. "No, because you obviously weren't actually there to get a tattoo. How did they talk you into it?"

"Didn't, actually. Well, maybe they pricked my pride a little." She took another deep breath and looked him in the eyes. "I didn't want to blow my cover, but also ever since I saw it on you, it's become like a symbol of both freedom and safety." She shrugged. "Must seem silly to you, but I needed something to focus on while I was in there. Finding you was the only focus I had and this..." She gestured to her hip. "The only clue."

"Doesn't seem silly at all." He ran a finger over the label of his beer. "I got it to claim who I wanted to be."

"You wanted to be a warrior roaming the deserts after the apocalypse?" Her teasing tone brought a smile to his face.

"Not too far off." He didn't know why he felt the urge to share with her the truth he hadn't ever shared with anyone before. "I was a soldier who kept getting sent on darker and more dangerous missions. Undercover, like you, I had to do terrible things. Then one day I was ordered to do something that I knew if I did it I could never atone. So I blew up my world and started over from the ashes."

She reached out and gave his hand a squeeze. "You're a good man."

He smirked. "I thought I was a criminal?"

"That too. I'm learning the two aren't as mutually exclusive as I originally believed." Her expression said clearly her thoughts had gone to a dark place. He could only imagine how hard it was for a woman, who had believed in the system she worked for, to be betrayed. His own experiences might be darker than hers, but he had never been a true believer.

"This agent you think set you up, Victor Taylor. How certain are you he was the one?"

"As sure as I can be with no actual proof. One of the other

agents I worked with, Agent Devin, brought him in from the FBI. A week later my cover is blown to Hell, and the FBI is on hand to arrest me. Then there is the weird stuff I found on his computer."

"You hacked his computer?" Max was impressed. Nowhere in her file were any computer skills listed.

"No, I paid a lot of money for that program you so casually crushed." Cat shrugged. "It was plug and play. It would pull all Word, email, or other common readable files off a hard drive and copy them." She ran a hand through her hair, exhaustion plain on her face.

He was tempted to send her off to bed, but knew he needed this information. After she slept, her guard would be back up, and he wasn't sure if she would still be willing to share. "What weird stuff did you find on his computer?"

"Other than the files on the women and children, there were some financial things that didn't look right, but I haven't had as much time as I would like to dig into them." She took a long sip from her bottle. "Plus, have you seen him? He looks like the boy next door but wears a thick gold chain and a watch that costs more than some cars. Could be coincidence but I doubt it."

Max closed the distance, brushing her brown curls over her shoulder. The bruises from his teeth along her neck made his dick stand to attention, but he refused to give in to that side of himself again today. "Instinct is sometimes the only thing we have."

"That is all I've had for months." She looked up into his eyes. He brushed his fingertips along her jaw. She closed her eyes, leaning into his touch. "I'm tired."

"Let us handle this, Wildcat. I promise we will do everything in our power to get your life back."

"I can't." She shook her head and opened her eyes.

Of course she couldn't. He wouldn't be able to step back either if it was his future in the balance. Fuck if he knew how he was going to keep her safe and somehow involved. Whoever had done this to this vibrant woman would suffer if he had to drag them to Hell himself.

Chapter 13

I'd rather be a rider for a minute than a spectator for a lifetime.

Avery wouldn't admit it out loud, but sitting on the cold metal bleacher felt wonderful against her sore bottom. How crazy was her life that she, a wanted criminal, was sitting out in public at a charity motocross event? To make it worse, the men around her were people she would have gleefully arrested only a year ago. Coming here hadn't been her idea. Watching men do insane stunts on bikes might be fun, but she'd rather be spending the time trying to clear her name.

Unfortunately, the only options Max had offered her that morning had been, come or be locked in a secure room for the day. The idea of being trapped in a small room for hours made her stomach roll. As Avery looked over the crowd, she didn't know if she wanted to throttle Max for delaying her mission or admire his dedication to his commitment to the children's charity this event sponsored. Her feelings for the frustrating man were like a rollercoaster, constantly shifting and uncontrollable.

Like last night when he hadn't tried to make a move on her, she thought he was charming. The attraction between them was so strong that it wouldn't have taken much to convince her to start round two. Logically she knew getting a good night's sleep was important, but her hormones disagreed. Then he went and ruined all the positive feelings by telling her that until they had better information she was on lockdown and had to do exactly what he said.

She snorted. As if she was some meek sheep that was simply going to follow blindly along. As soon as she got the information they promised to give her, if they even had it, she would leave. No matter how great the sex or how sweet the man seemed, nothing was worth turning herself into something she was not.

"How's the hip, beautiful?" Ink, her tattoo artist from yesterday, strode up the bleachers with a cocky smile on his face. Following him like a shadow was Hannibal, his gorgeous ebony face set in a slight scowl.

"Fine." She looked away not wanting to talk to the men who had been part of tricking her. She had spent long minutes that morning looking at the tattoo on her hip. It was beautiful, even without color to bring it to life. Would she ever get it finished? Probably not. She doubted after she left he would be interested in doing anything more for her.

Hannibal snorted. "Fine. The word that every woman uses to mean anything but." His accent was like molasses melting on a summer day. It was annoying that someone she didn't like could sound so sexy.

"Are you mad at us, Sunshine?" Ink sat next to her with a wink.

Anger burned up her spine. "Why would I be mad at you?" She made her voice light and sickly sweet. "You tricked me into going back to your *Club*. Where I'm now a hostage. I mean it's every girl's dream to have all her freedom removed and get dragged to some weird charity event rather than being locked in a closet."

Hannibal's deep chuckle vibrated against her skin. "He threatened to lock you in a closet?"

"Close enough," she growled.

Ink nudged her shoulder with his. "It's a good cause. Max is the main attraction and always brings in a large crowd. If he wasn't here, there are lots of young'uns who would be mighty disappointed."

She understood that. And the fact that she seemed like the bad guy for complaining only made her more frustrated. Juvenile diabetes was an amazing cause, and it surprised her that these men cared so much. Oh sure, she had heard of bikers doing rides for charity, but this was the first time she had learned of an event like this. It was beautiful and she would have enjoyed it so much better if she wasn't being guarded by over muscled bikers to make certain she stayed put and behaved.

"Are you guys making Cat feel welcome?" Tari glided up the steps, her peasant skirt and blouse flowing in the wind. The woman's outfit was completely out of place for the outdoor track. Her black leather vest proclaiming her 'Property of Dragon' another oddity. Most of the crowd was in jeans and t-shirts, but somehow Tari made it work. A little girl with gorgeous midnight hair and sparkling brown eyes clung to her leg as she looked curiously around her.

"Of course we are." Ink leaned forward, his smile widening. "How are you today, Lali girl?" The little girl who looked to be about three waved to Ink, then blew him a kiss. To Avery's surprise, he reached out as if catching the kiss and pulled it to his heart.

"What are you doing, *mi Reina*?"

It took a moment before the Spanish endearment sank in. My queen. Val's use of the queenie nickname last night now made sense. The man coming up three steps behind Tari was a giant. Almost six inches over six feet, he towered over everyone including Tari who had to be five ten. The two were a gorgeous couple. His sharp Native American looks a beautiful complement to her regal Egyptian features. It was easy to see the adorable girl was a mix of these two unfairly attractive people.

"I was going to sit and talk with Cat for a bit. Cat, this is Dragon, my Old Man."

Avery waved, not positive about how to act. Did everyone not understand she was a prisoner? The tall man nodded at her, then reached down and scooped the little girl up and onto his shoulders. The peal of laughter from the child was almost musical.

"Okay, I'm going to take Lali down to the fence and let her watch from my shoulders. Don't cause trouble."

Tari raised an eyebrow, and Dragon chuckled and bent to kiss her forehead. The love between the two was almost palpable in the air. Why couldn't she find something sweet and simple like those two had? Instead, she was drawn to complicated, frustrating, and controlling men. Well, one man really. While she had dated before, those men had been chosen more for convenience than any personality traits.

Dragon strode off, and Tari turned to Hannibal. "You two trouble-makers can guard her from further away. Cami is coming over and we're going to have some girl time."

"There is nothing you girls can talk about that we haven't heard or done before." Hannibal smiled a dazzling white charming smile that seemed to bounce right off Tari.

"That may be so. But if you men get Club business, we get girl business." Tari crossed her arms with an impressively serious expression on her face.

"That so, darlin'?" Ink asked. "And if we don't want to go?"

Cami popped up from underneath the bleachers and startled Avery. The crazy woman in a full leather catsuit squeezed through the gap at her feet and up and onto the metal bench in front of her. "I t-tell Pixie you're being m-mean and you never get to taste her cornbread again." When she turned Avery saw the woman was also wearing a vest that matched the other Dark Sons, but hers read Property of Tek.

"Now that is just cruel!" Ink clutched his chest. "All right ladies, we will move away so you can chat, but we can't go far."

The two men moved further up the bleachers. Giant trees loomed above the bleachers, making an interesting backdrop for their retreat. Like nature itself was boxing in the arena and providing shade for the spectators.

This entire section of seating was reserved for the Dark Sons, so in a packed event they actually had a small amount of privacy. The crowd was loud as the sounds of motorcycles revving to life filled the air.

"We've got a little t-time before the race starts so l-let's talk." Cami rubbed her hands together with a strange glee in her eyes. "What's it like being a spy?"

Avery laughed. She shook her head, surprised she could find anything funny under the circumstances. This woman was such an odd mix of innocence and mischief. It was tough to think serious thoughts around her. She looked between the two women, uncertain what to say. Tari winked and gave a look that said clearly *Sorry for my crazy friend*.

Avery shook her head. "I wasn't a spy. You make me sound like I was James Bond or something."

Tari sat on the bleacher next to her. "You'll have to forgive Cami. She has a very active imagination. She's probably trying to come up with a new roleplay for her and Tek to try out in the bedroom."

Cami gave a cute pout. Her purple hair falling into her face. Avery didn't want to like these women, but it was hard not to when they seemed so genuinely interested in her. Taking a deep breath, she thought about what she was comfortable sharing.

"Undercover work, at first, is really unglamorous. Acting like a junkie to make a buy or to get in with other drug addicts to find out who the suppliers were in the area." People didn't really understand how hard it was to fit in with people like that. You had to lose yourself in the identity of an addict. Sit back and watch while people destroyed their lives and do nothing because you needed to gain their trust. "I did enjoy being Trisha though. My cover was as a rich daughter of a dead Cartel man. I dressed in expensive, gorgeous clothes and wined and dined people. I had to appear successful and in control to get them to trust me with their money. Unfortunately, no matter what you are wearing, the men in that world don't respect women. Holding my tongue at some of their sexist comments took willpower. What I wanted to do was smack them in the face."

Cami's eyes glittered with excitement. "That sounds amazing. W-Well not the junkie part but the losing yourself in a r-role."

Avery gripped the bleacher, trying to hide her frustration. Did this woman really think undercover work was a game like acting on stage? "It's not the same as roleplaying. If you, or anyone else messes up it could mean your life, as I almost learned the hard way." She didn't enjoy thinking about it, but someone giving away her identity had destroyed her whole life. It had taken some time, but she had realized she would probably never go undercover again, even if she got her life back. How could she trust it wouldn't happen again?

"T-true."

"We didn't ask for alone time with you so Cami could grill you on your past life." Tari put a gentle hand on her arm as if she could sense the chaos swirling in Avery's head. "I wanted to make sure you were okay. When Cami finally told me your story, I was angry they had tricked you. Being with someone in the MC is hard enough without starting with lies and deception."

How was this sweet woman part of this crazy group of people? Yeah, lies and deception did make things a little hard to swallow. So did the fact she was a captive. It didn't matter that she didn't have anywhere else to go. Being robbed of choice chafed against her skin like sandpaper.

"I'm not with anyone in the MC. Max is just helping me clear my name."

"You d-don't think you're with Max? I th-thought he claimed you in the basement."

"Claimed me?"

Tari's lips tightened. "We thought you had accepted his offer to be his Old Lady. Pixie overheard Sharp talking about your encounter in the basement. Sounded like the usual ceremony if not as public as some are." She gave a meaningful glance at Cami. "Usually Val has the 'Welcome to our Club' speech with new women. But Dozer has become overprotective in her last month of pregnancy. Pixie couldn't bring her son because he's so young. So they asked us to answer any questions you might have."

Avery winced and could only imagine what they had heard. She knew men were as bad of gossips as women. It was embarrassing to picture what they had said about her epic failure of reason. How had that been mistaken for some sort of induction into their Club?

"If you don't mind me asking, what is the usual ceremony for being made an Old Lady?"

Tari coughed and Avery was sure if she could be blushing, she would be. "Usually a Brother claims a woman in front of at least five of his Brothers and she accepts."

It was adorable that Tari was embarrassed about a conversation she had started. Avery crossed her arms. "By claim I'm assuming you mean fucks?"

"Doesn't have to be b-but yeah that is usually the way." Cami at least didn't seem the least bit embarrassed.

Avery frantically searched her memory of last night. It was hazy from the wild and heated exchange. "But the woman has to accept, right?" She did remember him saying she was his, but had she accepted his claim? She didn't think so.

Cami screwed up her face in indignation. "Of course. What w-would be the point of taking an Old Lady wh-who wouldn't be loyal?"

Avery shook her head. "You know you all sound like a cult?"

Tari's peal of laughter was musical, like her daughter's. "I suppose it does, but we're a family who looks out for one another. There isn't a man or woman in the Club who wouldn't drop everything to help another member out." Her face grew somber, losing the sparkle from her eyes. "I grew up in a religious commune that was more of a cult than anything else. They didn't care if any of the individuals were unhappy or hurting. They only cared about the leadership and their twisted sense of right and wrong. The Dark Sons only care if their people are safe and happy. The rules can be stifling at times but in the end I believe it is worth it."

"Rules?" She wasn't good with rules.

Tari folded her hands in her lap. A gentle smile tipped her lips upward. The woman gave off this sense of calm that was almost contagious.

"From the outside it looks worse than it is but there are actually very few rules. The Club comes first. The men can't always talk about what is going on or what they are doing. You have to show respect to the Brothers and if they give an order, you follow it without question. Oh, and you don't share Club business with Civilians."

That sounded awful, but it would be rude to say so when she seemed so calm about the whole thing. "So you get ordered around and have to obey?"

Cami shrugged. "Technically yes. But no one has ever given me an order that w-wasn't for my own safety. I've h-heard of clubs wh-where the rules are used to abuse their women, but that is not the c-case with the Dark Sons. And while we don't argue in public, in private I know we all have had a word or two w-with our men if we didn't agree with something they do or say. But the structure, family, and sense of purpose you get, can't be found anywhere else. Our men love us with all their hearts and souls and don't h-hesitate to show us how they feel."

"And it doesn't bother you they can't talk to you about what they are doing?" Avery winced at her confrontational tone, but why did these women take all of this so meekly? They didn't seem like the types willing to bow down and scrape to their men.

Tari gave her a censuring scowl. "If you were working undercover could you have told your boyfriend what you were doing?"

Okay. She had a point. "No. That's true. What about the fact they do illegal things?"

Cami snorted, and Avery remembered she was a hacker who probably didn't have much respect for the law. "Th-they have their own laws and follow them. Is it optimal that they could end up in j-jail for some of the things they do? No, but our m-men are smart and don't take unnecessary risks. I prefer to focus on the good they do."

It was a slippery slope talking about the good outweighing

the bad. One she had been falling down for almost a year. She dropped her head to hide the emotions swirling through her head. Who was she to question if breaking the law bothered people?

She didn't wish to be a hypocrite. Breaking and entering might have been a victimless crime, but robbing the drug stash houses wasn't. On her last crime spree, she'd shot a person in the leg. Sure, he had attacked her, but she had been emptying the safe. It was only luck he hadn't died. Her own justification that they were criminals didn't appease her conscience when she thought of how much worse it could have been.

It would be hard, but she needed to adjust her thinking. She wasn't any better than any of these people and was probably more criminal than some. Avery wiped her hands on her jeans.

"So I'm guessing this means you aren't Max's Old Lady?" Tari's quiet question held weight.

"He never asked me to be his Old Lady." Had he?

Cami cocked her head. "And if he d-did?"

Did she want him to ask? Their chemistry was off the charts, but not something to build a future on. Would it be nice to have someone as strong and loyal stand by her side? Sure, but they barely knew each other. Thinking about a commitment, these people thought of as more sacred than marriage, was ridiculous. Wasn't it?

"I'm attracted to him. What else is there to say? I know nothing about the man except that he has mad fighting skills, rides a motorcycle for fun, and saves women from slavery in his free time." And he made her body ache for him with a simple look.

"I guess I w-wanted something good for him." Cami sighed. "He's had a rough life. Maybe it's s-silly but since you were a spy too, I thought you'd understand him."

Cami's words sparked her curiosity. "A spy too? What do you know about Max? He was a spy?"

Tari gave her friend a disapproving frown. "Cami."

"I know. I kn-know." The purple haired woman sighed. "All I'll say is his story makes yours look like a light children's novel. If he ever tells you even a small portion of it, consider yourself lucky. He doesn't share his past with anyone."

"Then how did you hear about it?" Her stomach burned, and she clenched her fists. Jealousy wasn't something she should be feeling, but her emotions overrode her logic.

"I met Max a long t-time ago under a different name. Before he was a Dark S-Son. He wasn't very nice to me, and well, I might have p-plotted revenge." Cami shrugged. "But when I looked into him and what he'd had to do for his country, I couldn't do it. I'm glad I didn't because the man he is today and the things he's done since, more than makes up for what he did to me."

Avery was hit hard by the raw emotion she felt in the woman's voice. She had to admit, if only to herself, that she wanted to know who Max was, both past and present. She had placed him in a box, a very sexy and tempting box. Nonetheless, she had judged him without all the facts. Yes, she would give him a chance, even if it meant breaking her heart later.

Chapter 14

Sometimes you have to risk the fall to know how it feels to fly.

Max slid his bike to a stop in front of the stands and waved to the crowd as his pulse settled in his chest. He had made it through another event and had landed every trick perfectly. Pitting himself against others in a straight race was fun, but the freestyle events at motocross was his true love. Just him, his bike, and whatever crazy stunts he felt like trying. This event was an exhibition, not a competition, and he had managed five different flips, choosing ones that had more flash than difficulty. From the sound of the crowd, he had chosen well.

One of his crew came and took his bike from him. He strode over and jumped the fence where his Brothers and their families were all gathered. He took a moment to enjoy their approval. Several Brothers smacked him on the back and teased him about the insane tricks. He moved through them with purpose, focused on one person. His Wildcat was sitting up in the bleachers with Tari and Cami. Why hadn't she come down to the fence like everyone else?

What would she think of the show? To say she hadn't been thrilled by being forced to come today would be an under-statement. If it hadn't been a charity event, he would have skipped it. Bailing on a commitment like this wasn't something he was willing to do. Despite her anger, he hoped she had enjoyed herself. Never before had he cared what people thought of his hobby. Would it bother him if she hadn't enjoyed herself?

He had barely broken through the crowd when Tek grabbed his arm. "Hey Brother, great ride."

"Thanks." Max turned away, not wanting to be rude, but he needed to talk to Cat.

"Got something for you on your girl I don't think can wait."

Max stopped and turned back to face his Brother. Tek was an oddity among the Dark Sons. He dressed like them, hung with them, but somehow never let the darkness show. It was something in the way he held himself that just shouted respectable and clean cut. The joke was on anyone who fell for that appearance, as he was one of the kinkiest twisted individ-uals Max had ever met. The fact that his Brother's face was set into serious lines tripped all of his warning alarms.

"What do you have?" With the adrenaline already rushing through his system, it was hard for Max to figure out if his racing pulse was nerves or from the let down from the run.

Tek ran a hand through his blond hair. "Ran your girl's info along with all the players in her life through my usual systems and didn't come up with anything new."

"Okay, I thought you said you had something."

"I do. But you need to keep this tight."

"Of course." What the hell kind of secret would have him asking for his silence? As Officers in the Dark Sons, they were both privy to information that wasn't for common consumption.

"You know my girl has sources that are above and beyond the usual. She designed software custom tailored for our use. The program searches the information she knows about on the dark web but she also created a searchable file system of government files she has obtained. The database holds information on every Brother's past that would make The Pentagon jealous. Of course she won't even let me access the raw data. Only her program can search it looking for common threads in our histories with any data put into it. It then tags that Brother's name as a match."

"Does it say why they are connected?" How much of his past had Cami put into those files?

"No, all you have is your original data and a Brother's name. I'm sure Cami could pull it out but she says it would be an invasion of privacy." Tek shrugged. "My woman has a very odd set of ethics for a hacker."

"Okay. I guess I can see her point. So what does this have to do with Cat? Do any of the Brothers have a connection to someone in her files?" Max stepped back and tried to think. He couldn't believe that one of his Brothers would be involved in destroying a woman's life without an excellent reason.

"The program flagged you."

Ice poured across his skin. "What data set off the flag?" His past was filled with some of the worst people in the world. Twelve years undercover in at least three major criminal organizations meant there was a wide field of scum to pick through. At thirty-eight he had enemies on both sides of the law who would burn down his life no matter what the cost if they realized he was still alive. The only reason they didn't haunt him now was he had headstones in four different countries, the last one with his birth name on it in Arlington cemetery.

"Agent Victor Taylor." Max recognized the name of the lead FBI agent on Cat's case. "The usual checks said he was squeaky clean. So I ran him through Cami's program." He pulled his phone out of his pocket and scrolled. He turned the screen around. "Do you know this guy?"

At first the man with slicked back brown hair on the screen didn't register. He looked like any mid-level bureaucrat anywhere. Then something about his sharp nose sparked a memory. Recognition hit Max like a bullet through the kidney. Take twelve years off the face, add a spiked up haircut, gaudy clothes and ridiculous gold chains around his neck and you had Viktor Gunav, bastard son of one of the most powerful men in the Borisyuk Clan.

"Fuck." A stream of memories played through his mind. Alcohol, drugs, women, violence and so many more terrible things done for the name of moving up the chain of command.

Max rubbed his chest. Several of his tattoos were coverup work hiding the evidence of his sins during his years in Russia. What was the spoiled boy, who could never make his papa happy, doing working as an FBI agent? If he had his sights set on Max's woman, what the fuck did that mean?

"I take it you recognize him." Tek tucked his phone back into his pocket. "I know you don't talk about your past, but is this something we need to worry about more than the usual?"

"I'm not sure. He was a low level player when I knew him. An easy way into the inner circle of the Stepanov Bratva. He was family, but from the wrong side of the tree. I would never have expected to see him in America."

"We need to pull in Hawk. If this is going to put us on bad footing with any of the Russian mafia families, then he needs to be told."

"Yeah. Not what I needed right now. Fuck, if he's after her, the man has resources we weren't planning on. I thought she only worked the cartels. Why would the Russians be interested in seeing her dead?"

"I don't know, but you better put your game face on. Here come the ladies."

Max looked up and watched the women walk down the steps of the bleachers. Cami was in some ridiculous leather jumpsuit that made her look like something out of a spy movie. Tari was pretty, as always, in her hippie-like clothing. Cat in tight jeans and a fitted t-shirt looked better than she had in the short skirt and crop top she'd worn at the tattoo shop. Her sleek grace as she walked had everything below his belt, standing up and paying attention.

Staying away from her was going to be an impossibility when everything in him was excited by her. He loved her fire and martial skill, her fearless personality and bratty mouth. It was like the woman was specifically designed to distract him. Now that she was in danger from someone in his past, there was no way he would let her go anywhere until she was safe.

The women reached them, but instead of stopping Cami walked by bumping Tek with her shoulder. "Sorry." Her teasing tone didn't seem like she was sorry at all.

Tek reached out, grabbing her wrist. He pulled her in front of him with a grin. In her fingers was Tek's phone. His brother raised an eyebrow and reached behind his back, pulling out a set of police style handcuffs. Max chuckled as his brother quickly took his woman to the ground and had her hands cuffed behind her back.

"Get off me, Pig. My hand slipped. I wasn't going to keep it," Cami protested.

It was a testament to how often those two did strange and kinky things that after a glance and laugh all the crowd of Brothers went back to what they were doing.

Max shook his head. "You should get more lessons from Pixie before trying out that trick again." Cami scowled at him.

"I'm going to take you back to the office and ask you some questions, little thief." Tek's voice was serious and Max had to admire the man's imagination and commitment to their sexual games that he never missed a beat. "You got this?" Tek nodded to Tari and Cat.

"Yeah, we're good."

With that his Brother lifted his struggling woman off the ground and threw her over his shoulder, striding off towards the garage. Cami's kicks and curses didn't slow Tek down at all.

"Shouldn't we do something?" Cat gestured at the leaving couple.

Tari laughed. "That's her Old Man, Tek. You'll get used to their unique love story. At least she didn't choose to be anything really unusual today. I suppose it's because she knew kids would be here."

"That's toning it down?" Cat's expression was an adorable mix of shock and horror.

"Yeah, well you saw her slave girl outfit last night."

"Right."

"She goes full in on whatever character she is playing no matter the audience." Tari chuckled.

Seeing her bonding with the other Old Ladies gave him a warm feeling. Why couldn't they have met under normal circumstances. Then he wouldn't be forced to cut short her fun.

"You mind giving Cat and me a few minutes?" Max asked. Tempting as it was to put things off, he needed to have a conversation with Cat.

"Not a problem." Tari bent down and gave Cat a hug. "It was good talking to you."

Max was fascinated by the way Cat's face transformed as Tari walked away. Her eyes narrowed, lips thinned, and muscles tightened until she was the picture of annoyance.

"You just love that, don't you?"

Max crossed his arms, interested to hear what had gotten her all riled up. "Love what?"

She rolled her eyes. "Women jumping to obey your orders."

"Hmm." Max stepped closer, loving the way she stood her ground. "If you think that was an order I think you've lived a very sheltered existence."

"Is that a joke?" She tilted her chin up in defiance, causing his dick to jump to attention.

"Orders aren't phrased as questions, Wildcat. You'll know when I give you an order."

"And you'll just expect me to obey?" Her tone held annoyance, but her pupils were wide with arousal.

He couldn't resist running a thumb over her bottom lip. "If it's for your safety, yes, but if you haven't noticed I like my women with some fight in them. Makes their surrender all the more sweet."

Chapter 15

Poking the bear might be dangerous, but it sure can be fun.

A very wet her suddenly dry lips. She didn't even understand why she was goading him. Watching him fly and do flips on his bike had been one of the most exciting experiences of her life. The way he filled out the racing shirt and pants was sexy as hell.

Confusion at her lust-filled reactions to him made her angry. She had two options, jump him physically or verbally. Maybe she should have simply kissed him. It would have been easier than trying to argue while her body was screaming for attention.

"I don't surrender." Well, she hadn't ever before. The temptation this man represented was frustratingly hard to ignore. Her nipples tightened at his knowing look and she crossed her arms trying to hide the evidence of her inappropriate arousal.

His chuckle was dark and did all sorts of wonderful things

to her body. "You surrendered beautifully last night." She would have argued, but his thumb over her lips held her quiet. "I think you want to be ordered around, Wildcat. I think you'll argue and bite and growl. But in the end you'll enjoy following every order I give because I'll have earned your submission."

She tried to bite his thumb, but he pulled his hand away with a chuckle. Why did his words strike a chord deep in her chest? The idea of submitting blindly to someone didn't appeal, but if he earned it?

That was what had made last night something unforgettable. He was able to take her on full force. She didn't have to be weak for him to be strong. What would it be like to give over to this man for even a night?

She stepped back shaking her head, unwilling to think about it. "You didn't ask Tari to leave so you could spout nonsense did you?"

His lips tipped up in a smile. "No. I wanted to ask you some questions and share some information with you."

Had he gotten the information she needed? The thought was both exciting and disappointing. Avery thought she would get more alone time with him to work out the lust between them before going their separate ways. But if she had the opportunity to clear her name, it was worth any sacrifice. Her pulse raced and her hands trembled.

"Did you find the information I was looking for?"

Max shook his head, and her stomach dropped. Of course, it couldn't be that easy. Why would she think things would go her way?

"Sorry, Cat. Not yet, but we did find some interesting things. What do you know about the Stepanov Bratva?"

"The Russian mob?" She tried to figure out what that had to do with her situation. "Not much. They aren't really part of the Denver drug scene outside a few designer drugs. I didn't have a reason to know about specific families. Why?"

"We have reason to believe they might be involved in the people still coming after you."

Avery searched her memories and came up blank. Because of her looks, she had been chosen to work mostly Mexican or Colombian contacts. There had been a few busts early in her career of college-level dealers, but nothing she could think of that would attract the attention of the Russians. Unless…

"Was Mitchel Thomas connected to the Bratva you mentioned?"

Max's face went still, and he took a few seconds to answer. "He was an information broker and human trafficker." It didn't look like he was lying, but she was sure it wasn't the full truth. Why the hell was he acting cagey?

"So is that a yes?"

Max gave an annoyingly noncommittal shrug. "He had ties to criminals internationally, but wasn't specifically tied to any one organization."

Excitement tickled her stomach. "So that could be it. How do you know the Stepanov Bratva is involved?"

"Doesn't matter."

Avery's face flushed as anger replaced excitement. "Doesn't matter?" She shoved his shoulder. "This is my fucking life we are talking about. You will fucking tell me everything."

Frustration roiled in her chest. The ups and downs of the last year too much to handle calmly. He stood there looking angry, as if he had the right. He was keeping information she needed from her. This year, this month, hell, this day was too much.

Everything was out of her control. The scream of rage that she had held inside too long, burned at the back of her throat. How dare he keep things from her? How dare the world do this to her? She had played by the rules her whole life, and where had it gotten her? She lashed out with another shove, knowing he wasn't really her enemy but unable to stop herself.

Time seemed to skip and somehow she found herself chest to chest with Max. Her arms pinned behind her back. Her panting breaths mingled with his as they stood face to face. His eyes burned into hers with barely controlled emotion.

"Let me go." She struggled against his hold. The scream she was fighting to contain echoing in her words.

"If you hit me, Wildcat, it better be foreplay." He leaned in, sharp pain shooting through her as he bit her earlobe. "I may find it sexy as fuck, but do not mistake me. Do it again and you will end up underneath me begging for my cock."

Her pussy clenched at his sexy words. She had never struck a person in frustration. Something about her situation had turned her almost feral. He was the perfect target. Someone strong enough to take what she needed to vent. Turn it into something better, something primal. She snapped, letting go of even the pretense of being in control.

She bit his neck hard. He let go of her hands and pulled back with a shout. She sprinted away, needing to run. To get free of the crowd.

Dodging startled spectators, she slipped through the people gathered around the side of the bleachers. A man grabbed her, pulling on her shirt. She struck out with an elbow as she broke away and ran. Max would be chasing her, and she didn't want him to catch her too quickly.

She jumped a log, then pushed through some bushes and found herself in the woods surrounding the arena. Her heart raced in her throat as she ran. Avery needed to let out the energy that had been locked up inside her for too long. It didn't matter where she was going as long as it was away from the crowds. Somewhere that she didn't have to hold back or be in control.

He was going to come after her. Avery couldn't make the

chase easy on him. At the same time, she needed him to capture her. Her arousal rose quickly, joining her anger in an intoxicating mix. The sound of footsteps as they crunched over leaves echoed behind her through the woods, sending her pulse racing impossibly faster. A large tree loomed in front of her, and she dashed behind it.

A small clearing was on the other side. Here was the perfect place to make her stand. She turned, expecting to have to wait a few moments, but he was only thirty feet behind her.

Max was a vision of tightly restrained aggression. His short hair a wild mess from the chase. Avery tried to speak, but all that came out was a growl. It didn't matter. Words were insignificant. She let go of civilized thoughts and gave in to her instincts.

No more worrying about the past and future. With him she was able to exist only in the now. Max was powerful enough to take what she desired to give. His tight, chorded muscles were beautifully outlined by the race shirt he wore as he leaned forward.

His return snarl was deep and vibrated in the air. This was what she needed. Words wouldn't come to her, but she needed to tell him what she wanted. Actions would have to do. She pulled off her top and threw it roughly to the side. He echoed her actions, tossing his black motocross shirt to the ground. This was still too slow. Avery snarled in frustration as she wiggled out of the rest of her clothes. Her skin against his was the only thing that would satisfy her.

She watched as he tore off the rest of his clothes. Desire built as she took in the nail marks that crisscrossed Max's skin from their last encounter. Until those healed, no one could look at his chest and not know he was hers. Their fast breaths were the only sound in the still woods. Then he moved.

She clutched at his shoulders as he lifted her up off the ground. His mouth claimed hers, as she wrapped her legs around his waist. Pinpricks of pain skittered across her scalp as his hand fisted her hair, not letting her move. He claimed her with his tongue, brutal and raw. Sparks of desire lit up her body. Unable to do anything but hold on as they each tried to devour the other.

Avery's core dripped with excitement as she rubbed against his length shamelessly. Empty, she needed to be filled, but couldn't get the right angle to take him inside her. She growled with frustration and need, but words were beyond her.

His grip tightened as pulled her against him and strode the few steps to where his clothes lay on the forest floor. Why was he able to think? She bit at his lip as he laid her down on his clothes, the fabric a slight barrier against the hard ground. Finally he would ease the ache that had turned into a dull pain.

"Mine." His words rumbled against her lips.

He tore his mouth away from hers and nipped his way down her body. She shook with each tiny bite. Thrashing against his hold was useless as he kept her hips pinned with a powerful grip. When his mouth reached her core, lightning exploded behind her eyes as he nipped her clit. The scream that she had held back echoed off the trees as an orgasm wracked her body.

His mouth danced across every nerve in her pussy and forced her pleasure higher as he fucked her with tongue and fingers, not letting the orgasm fade but somehow building it higher. A second orgasm crashed over the first and her body gushed its release.

She clawed at the ground, needing to grip something as her body shattered in ecstasy. As the wave started to slow, she felt his body slide up hers and she opened her eyes to meet his gaze. Before she could relax, her hips rocked and finally, she was filled. Their kiss was electric as he thrust with sharp strokes of his cock. She moaned at the earthy taste of herself on his tongue as he thrust deep inside her, reaching depths only he had ever found.

It was as if their bodies became one, so close were they pressed together. Chests touching, she wished it were possible that they could sink further into one another with just a little more pressure. He fucked her in rhythm to their racing heart-beats as she clawed at his back, trying to get him closer.

His growls echoed her moans inside their kiss. Pleasure built at the base of her spine, and she knew this next orgasm would tear her apart. She gave over to the orgasm, needing to let out all her pent-up emotions. As she screamed her release into his mouth. She felt him follow her moments later with small brutal thrusts.

The echo of their breaths was the only sound she heard as they both lay motionless. This was the perfect moment where their inner beasts were both sated. As the adrenaline faded, she felt the press of rocks and twigs against her tender ass and squirmed. He might have tried to set them down on his clothes, but at some point during their wild fucking they had ended up on the dirt of the forest floor.

He rolled them over so she lay across his chest. Her body and mind felt at peace, even though she knew they would have to talk now. What the hell would she say?

Chapter 16

Forgive me, Father, for I have sinned, and sinned and…

The beat of Cat's heart against his chest slowed as they both caught their breath. Max felt the new scratches on his arms and back and couldn't hide the smile that pulled at his lips. He had been an asshole trying to hold back information from her, but he hadn't expected it to push her over the edge like that. It was habit not to talk about his past to anyone. The memories of those times were something he preferred to forget.

This beautiful wild woman deserved more from him. Though he couldn't regret the outcome. Never before had sex felt so raw. He was becoming addicted to his Wildcat. If he was going to keep her from running from him he was going to have to share and pray that the sins of his past didn't destroy the heat between them.

Max swallowed and gathered his thoughts as he stroked her hair. "I was undercover with the Stepanov Bratva for over two years." His words felt hollow but he forced himself to continue. "Back then they were closely tied to the Russian government and had access to information the US Government wanted badly. I was recruited for the mission because I had a flexible moral code, a talent for languages and accents and the physical skills criminal organizations needed." Or at least that was the polite version of what his files said. "I was told I should do what was necessary in order to move up in the organization."

Cat shifted against him, settling her ear onto his chest. He couldn't resist running a hand down her long hair again. The silky feel of it against his fingers calming and comforting.

"The man you know as Victor Taylor, was a punk nineteen year old named Viktor Gunav. He was my way into the organization. As the bastard son of the head of the Borisyuk Clan he would do anything to make his daddy notice him. I was to help him." Max took a deep breath trying to explain. "The Borisyuk Clan was high up in the Stepanov Bratva so helping him rise in power was a great way to get inside the organization without raising suspicion. Making friends with him was easy. Within months we obtained a reputation for brutality because that was the quality most prized by his father." Memories skittered across his mind. The bloody images of both innocent and guilty men were a slideshow of horror in his thoughts.

Cat's hand traced circles on his chest. Her breath warm against his chest. "You did what you had to do to complete the mission. I get that."

"Yeah." Max sighed. "Except I never got any information big enough to merit action. After two years the Stepanov Bratva fell out of favor so I was pulled for a different assignment. I did manage to kill a few of the low level scum with me when I faked my death but everything I'd done meant nothing except filling in a few blanks in some black files." He shook his head trying to push back his anger. "I don't know how Viktor ended up in the US or as an FBI agent but that man is a cold-hearted sociopath who enjoys hurting people."

Her hand settled against his chest, the warmth soaking into his skin. "So you think he's a Russian spy?"

"It's the only thing that makes sense. I still don't understand why he would go after you." Max enjoyed the glide of her skin as she shifted against him.

"I don't know. It's possible he was the one who set me up to begin with and was afraid if I was alive people might find out about his role in it. Maybe your people will find something more in the files I stole from him." She tilted her chin up and Max saw pain and exhaustion echoed in her eyes. "I'm sorry I pushed you."

He chuckled and shook his head. "Not the healthiest of reactions to being annoyed, but I get it."

"Do you?"

"It is human nature. Fight or flight. With what you've been through the last year, it's got to be hard not to see every situation as conflict. I don't ever see you fleeing, Wildcat, but I'm not the enemy. No matter how hot this was, we can't take a break to fuck it out every time you get angry."

She sat up, and he let her straddle him. Her gorgeous breasts a wonderful sight as she huffed, obviously annoyed. "That is only part of it. My whole life I've had to be less and somehow more than the men around me. It's frustrating. Work or relationships the double standard is stupid. When Tari and Cami thought I was your Old Lady, they gave me the run down on *the rules*." She shook her head. "I thought you were better than that."

Her position had the warm, wet center of her pussy pressing down on his cock. He couldn't stop his body from reacting to the magnificent woman on display above him. Max ran his hands up her thighs and pinned her hips in place so she didn't squirm making things worse. "Better than what?"

"Treating women like objects. I saw the property patches. Heard all about the *obey your man* rules." She leaned forward as much as he would let her to stare down at him. His dick pulsed. "I am not your *property*."

Max shook his head. "You say that word with such scorn, it is obvious you don't understand what it means." He tightened his grip, enjoying the way she softened into his hold. "Words only have the meaning we choose to give them. Did any of the Old Ladies you met seem abused or unhappy?"

"That's not the point." She rolled her eyes.

"Isn't it?" Max gave her his most serious stare. "When a Dark Son claims a woman, it means more than a Civilian marriage. It's not about material things like taxes, insurance or finances. She becomes part of the Dark Sons family. Someone to protect and cherish, no matter what. She gains hundreds of men across the country who will lay down their lives to keep her safe." Max sat up, the movement setting them eye to eye. "Does that mean she has to show respect to those men? Yes. Does it mean she has to follow orders to be sure they have the best possible chance to keep her safe? Also yes. So don't disrespect what you don't understand."

"Women are not less than men."

He slid his hands up her sides, and her breath caught in a beautiful shudder. "Never said they were. But we are different. Fair or not. In this life we lead, the men are responsible for protecting each other and the women. That is the way we choose to live. The women flourish under that protection not because they are weak, but because they are strong enough to let someone else help them."

He brushed his thumbs under her breasts with light strokes. Her nipples puckered into tight points. Max understood she was struggling with his words. It was a concept many people had difficulty with. Society taught that depending on others was a weakness, especially if you were a woman. Property meant something that was valued, something important enough to claim.

"But men don't need help? Someone to shelter them so they can flourish?" Cat's raised eyebrow was adorable.

Max cupped her cheek. "Of course they do. That is why we are a Brotherhood. True democracies don't work because individual fear often rules the will of the people. In an MC you have to give up that fear and trust in your Brothers. I have to follow orders, show respect, and put the good of my Club before myself."

Did she realize how she leaned into his touch, seeking more contact? Her mind might fight the concept of submission, but her body obviously yearned for someone to share her burden. He stroked her cheek lightly with his thumb. Max swallowed a groan as her hips shifted, rocking her against his cock.

She closed her eyes and her hips tilted. He slid in the honey between the warm folds of her pussy as she started a slow rocking motion. He hadn't thought he could be ready again so quickly, but something about her had his body primed for another round.

"What if you don't agree with the order?" A deep moan followed her words as the tip of his cock slid inside her.

It was hard to concentrate while she took him slowly into her depths. Max knew this was an important conversation and if she needed to be riding him while they had it, he wasn't going to complain. He slid one hand into her hair and the other around her hips, shifting so he could seat himself fully inside her. The motions were slow and deliberate. They needed to be joined as one so they could communicate on the most primal level.

"I can disagree. I have disagreed." He slid her up and down the length of his cock. "But in the end we have a chain of command and trust they know what is best for us all."

She relaxed into his grip, letting him move her with slow deliberate motions. Her nipples pebbled with excitement and rubbed against his chest with each thrust.

"And they'll never betray you? Never abandon you?"

The yearning in his Wildcat's voice was painful to hear. The connection of Brotherhood was hard to explain, but he tried. "They're human, so anything is possible, but there is a reason you can't join on a whim. By the time you have been a Prospect, you know what joining will mean. Not only the fun parts but the work it takes to be part of something bigger than yourself. And the Brothers have seen you in both good and bad times. It's an informed choice you make for life."

His thoughts scattered as she ground against him her pussy tightening. Her hands cupped her breasts in a tempting display. He wanted to bite down on her dusky nipples, but knew if he did this conversation would be over.

"For life seems like an unrealistic temptation and trap." Her breath was coming in short gasps.

Max was impressed she could think so clearly. The sensation of her riding his cock was a slow burn of pleasure that was going to end as explosively as their previous more energetic fucking had. He thrust up into her then held her tight, their bodies joined as closely as they could be.

"No one is held against their will, but the cost of leaving is high. Once you've known true acceptance, would you throw it away for some small disagreement?"

"No." Her answer was a small exhale against his lips.

It was like their souls touched, and Max knew she would be his salvation. Her wild spirit and fire would burn away the darkness he had been trapped in for so long. It didn't matter they had only known each other a short time. Instinct had kept him alive this far in his life and every cell of his being told him she was the one.

He didn't want to scare her, but he had never backed away

from a truth he understood so deeply. "If I claim you in front of my Brothers and if you accept, there will be no going back. You will be mine not just for the moment but for forever." He pulled back and thrust into her, that sound of their bodies meeting like a punch. "Remember that, Wildcat."

He took her mouth in a kiss that held all his banked passion. He tried to show her with every part of his body what his words couldn't. She melted into him and for one blissful moment he swore she fully gave over to him. Would she be able to accept him and everything that meant once she was no longer trapped by situation and circumstance?

Chapter 17

"We are not retreating – We are advancing in another direction" –
Douglas Macarthur

A very didn't think she had ever been so content
before. The word 'contentment' wasn't enough to
describe the peace and purpose she was experienc-
ing. It wasn't the ache of her well satisfied body or that they
were any closer to clearing her name. It was a sense that things
were under control and there would be a solution.

After her encounter in the woods with Max, they had
cleaned up and endured some good-natured teasing when they
rejoined the Dark Sons at the rally. Afterwards they had come
back to the compound to a BBQ already under way. She
looked around the large crowd of cheerful people with a touch
of awe.

Knowing the Dark Sons had over fifty Brothers was one
thing, but seeing them and their families bonding over beer
and good food was another. The sense of community and

camaraderie was something she had never seen in a group this large. If it weren't for the overabundance of tattoos, black clothing, and leather cuts, she wouldn't have believed it was a gathering of bikers.

"You look as wide-eyed as a minister's daughter at her first frat party." Val's southern twang broke her out of her thoughts.

Avery chuckled and shook her head. The gorgeous redhead was striding over to the table where she was sitting dressed in an emerald shirt that said *Partying for Two* in gold glitter over her large baby bump. Glad for the familiar company, she waved for the woman to join her.

Max had left her alone a little while ago to talk to some of his Brothers and she had decided to stay and people watch while she pulled her thoughts together. The next day they would put together plans about what to do about her situation, but they had both agreed to let it go for now and enjoy the nice day.

Val settled herself across the picnic table, a warm smile on her lips. "Not what you expected?"

"No. I was expecting more of what I saw last night at the Clubhouse. Drunk men, barely dressed women, maybe some fights. This is…" Avery wasn't sure how to describe it.

"It's family. Oh the boys get wild, no mistake, but not at family events." Val rubbed her stomach with a small smile. "My daddy used to say an MC needs three things to thrive. The wildness that calls them to the open road. The fight to protect and keep what they claim. And the strength of a solid home so they can rest their tired souls."

Her words were beautiful and seemed to wrap up everything Avery had been pondering. Max's words earlier had started her mental journey, but Val had summed it up much more succinctly. "I'm not a passive woman."

Val's loud laugh was completely uninhibited and filled with

a sense of joy. "No. I don't suppose you are. Is that what you think Max wants?"

Avery snorted, then raised a hand to cover her face in embarrassment. "No. I mean, I don't think so. We barely know each other." She shrugged. "We don't have any claim on each other. It would be foolish to think I knew him well enough to say for sure."

"Well, I've known him for years and I'll say he's never shown interest in a woman for more than a romp and the women he picked for that were, let's just say, troublemakers."

Heat raced up her spine as jealousy reared its ugly head. Why was she jealous of who he had been with? She had been planning on taking off as soon as her name was cleared. Had that changed?

"Has he been with someone lately? A girlfriend I need to worry about?" Her question was inappropriate, but Avery couldn't help but ask.

"No girlfriends ever, as far as I know." There was laughter in Val's eyes that made Avery have to admit how silly she was being. Saying in one breath she had no claim, but in the next acting the jealous lover.

"Sorry."

"Nothing to be sorry about, sweetie. I've seen it too many times to count. Our men are like tornados, sudden and wild. They sweep you off your feet in a moment and before you know it the world is a changed place and you are just trying to get your bearings."

"I don't know—" her words were cut off as the rock music that had been coming through the speakers cut off and was replaced by 'Highway to Hell' playing at a ridiculously loud volume.

Val stood, her head turned toward the Clubhouse. She looked back and shouted, "Come with me, Cat. No arguments."

All around her, people had started to move with purpose. The women were gathering up the kids and heading towards the houses on the other side of the enormous field where the party was being held. The men were all heading in different directions, but each looked like they knew what they were doing. What the hell was going on?

Val's grip on her arm snapped Avery out of her confused state. She followed the pregnant woman, scanning the area looking for Max.

"What's happening?" Avery was shocked at how fast the pregnant woman was moving. They were headed over to a gathering of women and children by the bouncy house set up in the middle of the large field.

The lighthearted gathering had, in moments, turned into a strange mess of controlled chaos.

"Police raid. That song means we don't have time to get people home so we change location. Women to the back of the compound."

Raid. The word sent ice racing down her spine. She needed to run. If the police caught her here, there would be hell to pay. None of these people deserved that. She looked around at her options. There were woods beyond the houses, the mountains in the distance, but she didn't have supplies. The police might already be watching the road, so that wasn't an option. What to do?

They came to a stop in the middle of a group of women most of them she recognized from her first night here. Val looked her up and down, a scowl filling her face. "Oh, I know that look. Don't you dare try to take off. Try it and I'll have these ladies tie you up like a spring calf at a rodeo."

"I wouldn't test her if I were you." Pixie stood in the center of the group of women, bouncing a fussing baby on her shoulder.

The loud music finally cut off, but the action around them

didn't slow. Avery shook her head. "They can't find me here. You all will get in trouble."

Tari placed a comforting hand on her shoulder. "You have Dark Sons' protection. That doesn't change when the pressure is on."

Shock and not a small amount of awe made her chest feel tight. She expected fear, anger, or at least annoyance from these people she had just met, but looking around she only saw one common emotion.

Determination.

"The guys are probably coming up with a plan as we speak." Cami shrugged. "But if not, we'll take you to my place, there is a secret bunker under it with all the luxury you could want to last a month."

Avery couldn't help her slack jaw. "But you don't even know me."

"Nonsense." Val waved a hand as if waving off inconsequential thoughts. "You're family, or will be soon enough. All right Ladies let's move this party to the other side of the houses so our men don't start worrying."

The roar of a motorcycle racing across the field had them all looking back towards the Clubhouse. A single rider sped across the grass, straight toward them. He wore a black full-face helmet but Avery would recognize that sure handling of a bike and lean muscular build anywhere. It was Max.

He pulled up next to them, not even kicking up dirt with how smooth his quick stop was. He held out a helmet to her and nodded to the back of his bike. A million questions flowed through her mind, but knowing now was not the time, she slammed the helmet on her head and scrambled onto the back of the bike.

"You ready, Wildcat?" Max's voice echoed in the helmet.

She couldn't resist a smile that no one could see behind her visor. "Yeah."

He must be able to hear her because they took off immediately. The momentum threw her back for a moment till she gripped her thighs and clutched his hips. Faster than she thought possible they were past the houses and on a dirt road heading into the forest.

"It's going to be a bumpy ride so hold on tight."

She gripped his hips a little tighter. Unlike their ride the other night, this one was bumpy and the seat occasionally smacked into parts of her still tender from their earlier games.

"What's going on?" She did her best to keep her voice calm.

"Agent Taylor got a federal search warrant for the main compound to find you. We don't know how he knew you were here but our man in the local police said they also have orders to detain for questioning several of the Old Ladies, myself and a few of the other Brothers who have been around you over the last 24 hours."

Ice settled into her veins as she contemplated what that could mean. A large metal fence appeared along the side of the road that must be a marker of the end of the compound. Up ahead a section of it was open, and she had to hold back a scream as the bike bucked as he drove off the road and through the opening. She looked back to see the fence sliding closed behind them like some secret gate.

Of course they would have a back way out. She held back her questions until they settled back onto another dirt road.

"What are you going to tell the police?" She hated the idea that this whole thing was her fault. The party ruined and the Club getting hassled.

"Nothing." His derision was clear.

"What do you mean, nothing?"

"You don't get it, Cat. I can't get taken in or questioned any more than you can. If Viktor recognizes me, a man who is supposed to be long dead, and starts asking questions, the wrong people will hear. People in our government who also think I'm dead though not for quite as long. That happens and my world implodes. Best-case scenario they put a bullet in my head to make my death a reality." His sigh was clear, even through the headset. "Hell, it may already be too late. If he has been surveilling the Dark Sons, he could have recognized me."

Guilt was like a fiery knife in her stomach. These men who had saved her not once but twice were going to end up paying a price they never bargained for.

"What about the others?" Her throat was tight.

Max's chuckle felt inappropriate. "Yeah, they're not going to enjoy that."

"You're chuckling over your Brothers being unhappy?"

"Oh, my Brothers aren't the ones going to be unhappy. Cami is one of the people to be detained."

She wanted to smack him and would have if she didn't think it would make him wreck the bike. "Her pain is amusing to you?"

Max's laugh was full throated this time. "Oh, she's not going to be the one in pain. Believe me. She may look sweet or crazy depending on the day, but that is one scary woman. By the time she is done, she will have them all begging for forgiveness and praying they keep their jobs."

This whole situation confused her. What the hell kind of people had she gotten herself mixed up with?

Chapter 18

It takes a strong woman to admit when she is wrong and a rare man to be smart enough not to gloat.

Relief filled Max as he pulled out of sight into the open garage. The colonial house the enclosure was attached to was set far back in the woods. He hoped they would be safe here. The house was technically owned by a corporation out of Louisiana who ran programs that assisted veterans to reintegrate into society. In reality, Hannibal and Ink owned both the property and the charity, though neither of their names appeared on any of the legal paperwork.

It was the fall back location Hawk had chosen for them since with federal law involved it was possible they could and would get a warrant for any property known to be owned by any of his Brothers. Depending on how things went back at the compound, he might or might not keep Cat here for a while to let things calm down. If things got too hot, they would have to leave the state.

How had that asshole Viktor found out she was with them? The warrants were too specific to not believe the Club was under surveillance. At first, Max had thought they had been watched last night inside the Clubhouse. But if that was true there were two names missing from the list of people wanted for questioning, Pixie and Val.

When you removed those two ladies from the equation, it narrowed down the timeline. They must have been spotted at the rally. Which meant the agents had moved fast to get the court order. Hopefully, that meant they hadn't followed all the rules because Deep and Cheryl would rip apart shoddy police work. How much had the unknown surveillance seen? Physically he had changed much since his stint in Russia, but age and a less polished look might not be enough. If Viktor had pictures of him, would he recognize him as his old friend who was supposed to be dead?

"I can almost hear you thinking through the helmet speakers." Cat hugged him from behind. Max shook himself mentally. They had been sitting idling in the garage for an awkward amount of time.

"Just trying to get my head wrapped around the situation." He tapped her leg. "Swing off and I'll park the bike."

He needed to turn the bike around in case they needed to make a quick exit. The maneuver would be easier without a passenger in the small space. Max had only been to his Brothers' house a few times since it was far off the beaten track. Ink and Hannibal enjoyed the remote location surrounded by woods and rarely invited people over.

Once he had his bike turned around, he pulled off his helmet and tried to decide what to do next. They needed information quickly, especially if he was going to have people from his past hunting him. He led Cat into the house, mentally reviewing which of his contacts would be safe to reach out to.

The hallway off the garage was longer than he expected, but the kitchen, he remembered, was down at the end. If his memory was correct, the living room where he had hung out with his Brothers was out front and there was an office with computers on the other end of the house.

"I need to use the ladies room." Cat grabbed the handle of the door next to her.

"Of course it's—" her horrified gasp cut him off. Max looked over her shoulder and chuckled. The room exposed behind the door would be a shock to anyone who didn't know his Brothers well. The stunned look on her face was adorable. He hadn't thought she was someone easily surprised. It was no secret that Ink and Hannibal were kinky men. But he hadn't realized they had a BDSM playground in their house.

"What kind of pervert are you? We're on the run and you bring me to a sex dungeon?" Her raised eyebrow and challenging tone were erotic as hell.

"No." He did his best to hide his amusement, but her scowl said it wasn't working.

She crossed her arms, and he couldn't help but notice the way her breasts lifted. She stepped into the room and made a sweeping gesture that covered the large space. "Oh, I'm sorry, are you going to try to tell me this is an unconventional gym?"

Max leaned on the doorframe and took in what she was seeing. Damn, the kinky shit was obviously more than a hobby for his Brothers. Bigger than most living rooms, it was an impressive sight. One wall held floggers, whips, paddles, and some implements he didn't even recognize. A St. Andrew's cross was against the right wall. Chains, restraint points, a bed and a sex swing were all present, along with several chests and benches. He had seen BDSM clubs with less quality equipment than was contained within these four walls.

"I brought you to a house that has a sex dungeon. Which neither of us would have known about if you didn't assume you could open doors without permission." He couldn't resist a smirk. "Seems to be a habit of yours."

Max enjoyed the way she flushed with embarrassment. It was tempting to see if she might enjoy some of the equipment here, but he wouldn't use anything without permission and they needed to find out what was going on.

Movement out of the corner of his eye caught his attention, and he saw Hannibal in the kitchen looking unhappy.

"If it's not yours, then whose is it?"

Max stepped back into the hallway and nodded to his Cajun Brother. Cat's eyes went wide as she quickly exited the room and saw over six feet of pissed off man glaring at her from the kitchen.

"Sorry, Hannibal. I was looking for the bathroom." Her tone was somehow defensive and aggressive. As if she was blaming him for her invasion into his privacy.

"*Cher*, today is not a day to push me. I got a call that the police shut down my shop and took Ink away for questioning." His Louisiana accent did nothing to lessen the bite of frustration in his voice. "And instead of being able to go back him up, I have to help babysit you. Do I get a thank you for that? No, I get to listen to you judge my lifestyle choices."

The fact that Ink had been picked up wasn't good. Hannibal was normally calm and rational. As a sniper, he had patience that most men would envy. The only exception to that was when Ink was in danger.

"I'm sorry." She should have left it at that, but Max could see she wasn't going to. "I was shocked and shouldn't have said anything." She lifted her chin defiantly. "You have to admit that what you're into is outside the norm."

Hannibal gave his Wildcat a glare. "She who lives in a glass house shouldn't throw stones. You will behave with respect in my house or you will be punished."

His Wildcat had a nasty habit of lashing out when she was

scared or embarrassed. His Brother had probably triggered both of those emotions with his words. Hannibal's jaw tightened, but much to Max's relief he stayed silent. Silence was apparently not what Cat wanted, because anger sparked in her eyes. He needed to cut her off before she pushed too far.

Max stepped in front of the woman, about to throw a match onto gasoline. He leaned down, so they were eye to eye. "Wildcat. You are in someone else's home. You implied he was a pervert and now are about to throw attitude. Don't be a hypocrite. You and I both know you are far from vanilla. Apologize."

She reeled back and her angry gaze switched to him like he intended. "I didn't, I'm not—"

"Not into kinky shit?" Max cut her off. "The bruises on your ass and the claw marks on my body beg to differ. Apologize."

The struggle on her face mirrored the one probably going on in her head. When anger switched to embarrassment, then guilt, Max took a deep breath and stepped back.

"I'm sorry, Hannibal. If you want to go to Ink, you should. Don't worry about me." Her tone this time held a genuine apology and a hint of exhaustion.

Hannibal's body loosened slightly, and he nodded. "Not the way it works. I've got my orders." He gestured deeper into the house. "The guest bathroom is in the other hall first door on your right."

Cat headed in the direction he indicated, but Max took a moment to close the door before following. He clasped forearms with his Brother who was shaking his head.

"You always did like a feisty brat."

Max smiled. "You don't?"

"Hell no. I want a woman who enjoys her submission and blossoms when pushed to her very limits. Thank God, Ink feels the same."

"So the sharing isn't casual fun for you two?"

"Nope, if we find someone to settle with, and Lord knows that is unlikely with Ink, it will be someone we can love together."

His two Brothers had come up through the Rangers together and were closer than any bond of blood could make them. He respected their bond, but didn't understand the desire to share. Simply the thought of Cat with anyone but him made his blood steam. That thought gave him pause. He had never been the jealous type before. With everything going on, now wasn't a good time to start.

Cat walked into the kitchen, where Max and Hannibal had paused to grab a beer. The tilt of her chin and determination in her eyes said the trip to the bathroom hadn't erased her embarrassment or relaxed her temper. She stopped a few feet in front of his Brother.

"I want to thank you for letting us stay at your house, Hannibal." Her voice was the picture of respect, but somehow he knew she wasn't done. "If we're going to spend time together, I would appreciate you not calling me childish or derogatory names."

Max ran his hand over his face. That she wasn't screaming and technically was using a respectful tone was a step in the right direction, but he needed to break her of the habit of turning every conversation into a sparring match.

"What derogatory name did I call you, Cat?" Hannibal stared at his woman with a raised eyebrow.

She growled in obvious frustration. "I heard you call me a brat to Max. I am not a child."

Max chuckled. "Oh, he wasn't thinking of you as a child, Wildcat."

"What other kinds of brats are there?"

"It's a type of submissive, *cher*." Hannibal put his beer down and looked over at Max. "I'm going to see if we have any messages from Hawk. You can explain to your brat exactly what that word means."

Cat's drawn in breath was sharp, but he was proud that she managed to hold in the biting comment he knew was itching to come out of her mouth. She stayed quiet until they both heard a door close in the other room. "Asshole."

"Actually I think he is being very understanding, considering you have been nothing but attitude and sass from the minute you met him."

"Of course you take his side." The hurt in her voice was so much more than the encounter deserved, and Max remembered how little support the woman had received in the last year.

He walked around the kitchen island and wrapped his arms around her. She stood stiffly for almost a minute, but then leaned into his arms. She was a warm bundle against his chest and he wished more than anything he could take away her pain. "He really wasn't insulting you."

She looked up at him, and he could see the strain of events pulling at the corners of her eyes. "Then what did he mean?"

What was the best way to explain something that was something common within the lifestyle? "How much do you know about BDSM?"

"I don't know." She gave a slight shrug. "I saw those movies, the acting was bad and the plot as weak as the female lead."

Max laughed, agreeing with her opinion of the movies that were so popular among the vanilla and uninformed. "Yeah, that is not what I'm talking about. BDSM like anything in life is full of variety and unique personalities. Dominant or submissive isn't enough to describe what someone likes except in the broadest of terms of who wants to give orders and who wants to follow orders."

She turned in his arms and put her cheek against his

heart. "Guess I'm a dominant then. I hate being ordered around."

"I think you are lying to yourself, but let's try an exercise. What is more satisfying, watching your team succeed without you or succeeding yourself?"

She shrugged. "I'd be happy for my team."

He squeezed her. "But which is more satisfying?"

"I guess succeeding myself." She sighed, her breath warm even through his shirt. "That sounds selfish, doesn't it?"

"Not worrying about that right now. Okay, do you want praise for a job well done?"

"Who doesn't?"

"Last question. Which appeals to you more, knowing exactly what to do and how to succeed or having to figure it out yourself?"

"What does that have to do with dominance? Of course I want to know how to succeed."

Max brushed his lips over the top of her head. "See, we are all different. I can follow orders if I have to, but I'm happiest when I'm finding my own path. I couldn't care less if someone praises me and find ten times more joy in watching someone else succeed then in doing so myself."

She pushed against him with a light shove. "So you're better than me?"

Max pulled her back into his chest. "What is it with you and the better or worse comparison between everything? People are different, unique in so many ways. Man or woman, dominant or submissive, those are not the qualities that make a person better than another."

"Well I'm not submissive, I hate taking orders."

Max laughed and felt her smile against him. "Some subs love taking orders, but in my experience it isn't about that. It is about the freedom to not have to make decisions. The trust in another person to let them choose what happens." He looked down at Cat and waited for her to look up into his eyes. "Brats, in my experience, don't submit easily even to those they trust. Instead they fight playfully against following orders. Because it is a way to reassure themselves the dominant is strong enough, and cares enough to take them in hand, before following the dominant's direction."

Cat snorted and turned her face so her ear was against his chest. "So you think I'm *playfully* fighting against you and Hannibal to make you prove you are man enough to handle me?"

Max swatted her ass. "No. You don't trust either of us. A brat who is scared and doesn't trust the person giving orders lashes out like you did. It's their way of protecting themselves. If a person holds fast, doesn't lose their temper, or give up, they might earn some trust. If they don't, then it proves to the brat that the person wasn't worthy of time or respect."

She stilled against his body, and Max was glad she wasn't just lashing out. She was considering his words.

"I want to trust you." Her voice held longing that made him want to find all the people who had broken this woman's trust and make them suffer.

"I know that will take time. But I do need you to stop acting as if we are the enemy."

Over the last two days, her actions had told him clearly that no one had ever made it past her prickly armor. In moments like this he could feel the wonderful woman she was underneath all the anger and violence. He didn't want her to be weak, but if she kept on like she was going, she would mouth off to the wrong Brother. She needed to learn that she could be both strong and give over control.

"Orders from Hawk." Hannibal strode into the kitchen. "Agent Taylor is at the compound with the feds searching the woods with dogs. We need to search his place while he's distracted."

"I already searched his place." Cat stepped out of his arms, and he immediately missed the feel of her.

This was a risky plan, but if most of the Brothers were held up at the compound and others under arrest, Hawk must think it worth the risk. "I'm sure you did, but I know this guy and how he thinks. Or at least how he used to think. I don't like the risk of taking her into public. Viktor could have guys on the lookout for her."

"We're supposed to leave her here. Hawk is going to send over some Prospects who weren't at the compound to watch over her."

"Her is standing right here and is not going to be left behind."

Max wasn't thrilled with the plan either, but knew if he showed that at all the only way they would get her to stay here would be to tie her up. "Wildcat. You need to stop and think. There is a price on your head, and you are on the most wanted list."

Her growl was exciting, but he saw the moment she accepted their decision. He turned to Hannibal. "How long till the Prospects get here?"

Hannibal looked uncomfortable. "Should be an hour but Hawk said we can't wait."

Max cursed. "I'm not leaving her alone."

"I can take care of myself. I've been taking care of myself for my whole life."

Fuck, he shouldn't have pricked her pride. There were very few times when he questioned orders from Hawk, but this was going to be one of them. Max knew what a difference a second set of eyes and weapons could make in any situation. He hesitated before pulling out his phone. On the one hand he could ask to be able to stay until the Prospects arrived either pissing off Cat with his lack of trust in her abilities or making her demand to come with them.

Taking a deep breath, he tried to bury his doubts down deep. "You got weapons for her?"

"Sure, but is she going to shoot the Prospects by mistake?" Hannibal's tone said he was kidding, but his eyes made it clear he wasn't sure what she would do with a weapon.

"I'm not a complete monster. I'll only shoot the bad guys if they come." Her voice was slightly teasing and had lost the edge of hostility she usually used with Hannibal. "How will I know if they are Prospects?"

"They'll be wearing cuts." Max gestured to his own cut to make a point.

"You guys don't ever take them off?"

"Not in this kind of situation," Max said.

"And if someone shows up without a cut?"

They couldn't pretend that there would be any choice but violence if someone not from the Club showed up. The reality they had to accept was the types of people after her wouldn't respect anything but lethal force. While Hannibal pulled out several weapons from a chest behind the couch, Max made sure his expression showed that there was no joking in his following words.

"If someone not a Dark Son shows up. Kill them."

Chapter 19

Not all women are made of sugar and spice some are made of gunpowder and lead.

A very took a deep breath and tried to calm herself. Her whole body had been firing on overdrive since Max and Hannibal pulled out thirty minutes ago. She didn't need them to protect her. The feeling of safety she felt around Max was an illusion. This house was in the middle of nowhere and the people after her were busy elsewhere.

She looked around the room for something to keep her mind off the ticking minutes as she waited for the Prospects to arrive. Ink and Hannibal's house was full of items that should have been able to distract her. Where Max's place was filled with photos and memorabilia of motorcycles, gorgeous works of art filled the walls of this home. Each one would go for hundreds if not thousands of dollars and had probably been created by the men themselves. Much like in the tattoo shop, there was everything in the artwork from the fantastical creatures to paintings of objects so realistic they might easily be mistaken for photographs.

On the shelves there was also a lot of rope, whips, and western themed items that, from the photographs of him at rodeos, she supposed were Ink's. She remembered the neatly coiled whips in the room down the hall. Avery's cheeks heated over how she had reacted at first seeing them. With time to reflect, she could see that she might have overreacted to the room. What people did in their own homes wasn't her business as long as everyone consented. Lashing out was an instinct that had been ingrained over years. Weakness was something she couldn't afford to show. Foster care then becoming one of the few female DEA undercover agents had made that painfully clear.

Why was she now questioning her behavior? Max's words earlier had started an uncomfortable loop in her mind. Did she automatically assume that everyone was going to hurt her? That was as foolish as believing everyone was good. Was she seeing hostility where there was none and lashing out? She didn't think she was testing people, but it might be why she had no friends.

Honestly, it had been exhausting trying to prove herself every day, and that had only increased in jail. The last month in hiding had been both terrifying and strangely restful. Only having herself to worry about. No one to judge or prove herself to. She had missed the structure of knowing what she was supposed to be doing.

She sighed and admitted to herself that it would be nice if she didn't always have to be the one to figure out what came next. Give over the decisions and control to someone else. Someone she could trust. She wouldn't be able to give that sort of control over to just anyone. Could she see herself giving over control to Max?

Yes.

Every action the man had taken from the first time they met in that horrible basement had been to help her in some way. His strength was something she could depend on. Avery knew in her heart he respected her. The man hadn't questioned her ability to take care of herself when he had needed to leave. Instead, he made sure she had weapons to defend herself more effectively. He hadn't wanted to leave her. In fact, it was easy to see he wanted to stay behind and make sure she was safe. But he had his orders. He trusted her to do what was necessary. Now she needed to start trusting him.

The distant sound of a motorcycle shook her out of her thoughts. Avery grabbed the Ruger AR off the table and slid the rifle's carry strap over her head. She rushed to the open front window to get a look at who was coming. It was probably the Prospects Max had told her to expect, but there was no reason to take chances.

Hannibal had said there was only one dirt road leading to the house which would limit access. The only reason people would be on that road was to come here. The rest of the property was surrounded by thick trees and vegetation, so while someone on foot might approach it wasn't likely. Her heartbeat kicked up as the sound of the vehicle grew closer.

Avery spotted the rider and hesitated for a minute. Even at this distance she doubted the slender person on the sleek-looking motorcycle was a Prospect. She snorted as the shape of the person became clearer. Unless the Dark Sons let women into their ranks. She sighted down the rifle, conflicted about what to do. Max had said to shoot anyone not wearing a cut. Avery stood with a curse. She wasn't about to open fire on a stranger not offering violence. The woman could be Ink or Hannibal's girlfriend stopping by for a surprise visit. How would she justify killing an innocent to the men? Or to be more honest with herself.

Fuck. What was she supposed to do, they hadn't left her

with a cell or even their phone numbers to call? There was no way of asking for confirmation. The woman looked relaxed as she rode towards the house, not like she was sneaking or rushing to attack. Avery watch as she turned the bike to ride around the back of the house. Guess it was time to find out if the woman was a friend or not. Avery moved through the living room and kitchen and pushed open the sliding glass door. Not wanting to be caught off guard she held her weapon raised and aimed at the woman pulling up.

The woman slowed to a stop about fifty feet away. She shut off the bike, pulled her helmet off, and leaned forward with a smile as she placed it in front of her. The woman was gorgeous, honey blonde hair braided down her back. If it weren't for the light lines around her eyes that placed her in her late thirties or early forties, Avery would have said she was in her late twenties. Dressed in a tight black leather outfit similar to the one Cami had been wearing earlier, there wasn't an ounce of fear in her at having a gun pointed at her. This woman exuded confidence like Avery only dreamed of doing.

The visitor raised her hands with a smile. "Hello, Avery. Good to see Max didn't pick a damsel in distress."

"Who are you?" The fact this woman knew who she was with was a good sign, but not enough proof for her to lower her weapon. The woman had an accent Avery couldn't place.

"They call me Akula." The way she said her name made her sound Russian or Eastern European. Max had said Agent Victor Taylor was actually a Russian named Viktor Gunav. Was this woman working with him?

"That's nice. But who are you and why are you here?" Avery settled the rifle against her shoulder to make it clear she wanted an answer now.

"I'm here for many reasons. The one important to you is Hawk is special to me. So I am willing to help one of his Brothers' women if they are in trouble."

"You're Hawk's Old Lady?" This woman was crazy, which to be honest meant she fit in perfectly with the other Old Ladies Avery had met.

Akula winked. "Nothing so formal."

"So what, you're going to keep me company until the Prospects get here? Thanks, but no thanks. You can turn your pretty ass around and head out."

Akula's laugh was deep. "I like you. How much do you know about the man hunting you?"

What the fuck was this woman's game? "Why should I tell you shit?"

"Because if you are completely ignorant, this explanation will take much longer."

Fine, she would play along. Telling this woman what she knew wouldn't make things any harder. "Victor Taylor is a dirty FBI agent who helped Mateo Lopez set me up. Either he or the Cartel put a price on my head. Now I've got both the law and people looking to cash in after me."

"Interesting." The woman leaned forward, resting her arms on her helmet. "I think you know more than you say, but time is short so I will make things clear. The Cartel doesn't care about you. But Viktor, he cares very much. You are a loose end, an embarrassment who he has failed to take out three times. That is an unacceptable threat to his reputation."

"Yeah, don't really care. I'll happily threaten more than his reputation. He will not get away with killing my partner." It was just like a man to worry more about his macho image than the physical threat.

"You should care. He has upped the price on your head again and called in some family favors."

"Because he's afraid I'll expose him?"

"No." Her tone was so condescending, Avery gritted her teeth. "You can't prove anything. If you try you would end up back in jail where it is much easier to kill you. Your continued existence embarrasses him. He ordered your death and yet you live. It makes him look weak."

This woman knew way too much not to be involved. Avery moved her finger from the gun's guard to hover over the trigger. "So you're here to collect on the money?"

"If I was here to kill you. You would have never seen me coming."

"I think you should go. I'll protect myself until my backup comes."

The woman shook her head and swung her leg over the motorcycle. She stood and managed to look intimidating, even with a rifle pointed at her.

"No one is coming. The message sent to clear out your man was a fake. A Bratva hit team is on the way here right now. Five highly trained men to make sure you do not survive."

Who was this Akula? She talked about a bunch of trained killers coming like it was a normal day occurrence. Why was she even listening to this woman rather than shooting her?

"Why the hell should I believe you?"

"I want Viktor embarrassed, then dead. His boss Andrey has plans I don't want to see succeed. I'm not yet in a place to go up against him myself, but I can help you and Hawk at the same time." She shrugged. "Decide. They could be here in less than fifteen minutes and we should prepare."

Avery was sick of everything always spinning out of her control. She was trying to stay calm, but anger boiled inside her. What was the right decision?

"You're willing to help a complete stranger face off against a hit squad because, why? A complicated scheme to fuck with some guy named Andrey?"

"Yes. And Hawk would not be happy if you died, and he fucks much better when happy." Akula's lips twitched in an almost smile.

"You are nuts. Why tell me this?" Avery took her finger off the trigger, deciding that if this woman was telling the truth any help would be welcome.

"There is no one you could tell that would matter to me. Andrey knows I hate him but believes me to be loyal." She shrugged and stepped forward. "Enough about me. You are being tracked. The men coming after you are skilled, but not the best. If I was them, I would block off the road and come in by foot so you don't hear. So we have fifteen maybe thirty minutes before they attack." She reached into her pocket and pulled out a black box about the size of a cell phone, but thicker. "We need to remove the tracking device and set up in a defensible position."

Everything was moving too fast, and Avery wasn't sure what to think. This woman sounded so sure of herself, but every word out of her mouth was harder to believe. How the hell could someone have slipped a tracking device on her without her noticing? "What do you want to do with that?" Avery gestured to the box with her rifle.

"It is a detector. One of Viktor's men placed a tracker on you at the motorcycle show. I find, we remove."

This was crazy, but Avery followed her gut and lowered the rifle, letting it hang from the strap. The woman closed the distance and moved the box in sweeping motions around Avery's body. When it passed around her back, loud beeps emitted from the device. In less than five seconds, Akula had picked something off the back hem of her shirt and held it up.

A small disk less than a half inch around was in her fingers and she tossed it onto the ground. "We shouldn't break it yet or they will know something is up. How good of a shot are you with that?" The Russian woman nodded to the rifle in her hand as she slipped the detector into a bag tied down to the side of her bike.

"I'm not a sniper but I know how to use it." Her marksmanship during training had always been above average, but nothing special.

"Good. We should–" The rumble of a car coming up the road was unmistakable. Akula cursed in what Avery assumed was Russian.

Avery pulled her rifle back into her hands. "Guess we're going to need a new plan."

Chapter 20

Pride is the cliff from which many fools fall.

Max's mind was a jumble of worries as he and Hannibal rode down the highway. Front most was his annoyance that neither of them was wearing a Bluetooth unit, so communication of anything complicated was impossible. The ride gave him time to think, and very little was adding up. Why hadn't he asked more questions before they left?

Max took a deep breath and tried to unclench his jaw. He knew why. The need to show Cat confidence in his Brother's plan had been a stupid first priority. That focus meant he hadn't bothered to ask Hannibal several key questions. Who were the Prospects coming to guard Cat? Why had Hawk picked Hannibal and him for this mission? Not knowing drove Max to distraction.

The more they rode the more things didn't feel right. It wasn't that he didn't trust any of the Club's Prospects. But they had all been at the compound for the barbeque, so how were any of them going to break free past the police to come guard? What were they hoping to find at Viktor's house that was so important they had to go now?

Max checked his mirrors, making note of each of the cars behind them. Most were new, but two of the ones in the slow lane had been with them ever since they had pulled onto the highway. An SUV and a minivan. An obviously frustrated mother drove the minivan with several kids in the back. Behind her was a SUV, the driver, a male in his twenties was alone. It had been almost fifteen minutes, and even though she had barely been doing the speed limit the SUV hadn't tried to pass. Completely out of character for the majority of drivers.

There was a rest stop ahead. Max pulled alongside Hannibal and signaled he wanted to pull in. It would accomplish two things. He could get the information he wanted out of his Brother and find out if the SUV was following them. They pulled off onto the exit lane and his nerves fired as the SUV followed a little way behind. Max pulled up to the gas pump, tracking the car in his mirrors as it pulled into a parking spot at the edge of the lot.

"I see we picked ourselves up a tail. You think it's the cops?" Hannibal's voice was almost muffled by the loud engines of their bikes.

"I'm not sure. They picked us up less than five minutes from your place. It is too big of a coincidence."

"You sure about that? I didn't clock him till a few minutes ago when that soccer mom swerved while yelling at her kids."

"Yeah, I'm sure."

"What do you want to do?"

"This whole situation has the back of my neck itching. What did Hawk say for us to do exactly?"

"His email said they were on lockdown and to take the opportunity to scout the FBI agent's house. He would send prospects over to cover Avery but not to wait for them so we didn't miss our window."

Something was off. Actually, a whole-lot of somethings. "Did he say who he was going to send? I thought all the Prospects were at the Clubhouse earlier."

Hannibal's lips tightened, and he shook his head. "Damn, didn't think about that."

Max pulled his cell out of his pocket, dialing Hawk. It was a risk, but they needed to know if they had been set up.

"Hey Maddog, little busy here." Hawk's use of the wrong name signaled he was either not alone or they were being listened in on.

"Understood. Need a confirmation on your earlier email. You still want us going on a field trip?"

There was the sound of people talking in the background. "No." Hawk's voice sounded angry. "You and Elephant are supposed to be settled in watching a chick flick."

Fuck. "We got an email that you were sending some puppies over and to leave the chick flick at home." Damn it. If he hadn't been so concerned with Cat's reactions, he would have questioned the orders earlier. It was a fucking amateur move.

"I don't have any puppies to spare. Where are you? Scratch that, don't tell me." Max could hear the frustration pouring through the phone, matching his own. "I'm guessing you're not where you should be. Get back there and let me know what kind of mess we have."

"Got it. May have a clue tagging along behind us. We'll see what I can find out." Max ended the call.

"I'm sorry, Brother. I should have gotten confirmation that the email was legit."

He didn't have time for his Brother's apology. Rage boiled in his stomach as he throttled his bike and put it into gear. Seconds later he was racing around the pumps, heading right for the parked SUV. Hannibal only seconds behind him. It wasn't the smartest of moves, challenging a guy in a car when he was on a bike, but options and time were limited.

Max wanted to race back to the house and make sure his Wildcat was okay, but he needed to know the situation they would be riding back into. Cops or hitmen. It was even odds either way. As the face of the man behind the wheel became visible, Max had to bite back a curse. The blond muscle behind the wheel smirked at him as he approached. Pavel was one of the top enforcers for Andrey Petrov, the head of the Bratva in Colorado and the surrounding states.

Max had never interacted directly with the man before, because Hawk understood the risks and kept him in the background. That option was no longer available to him. This man would either recognize him or not. It didn't matter. Max was going to pull every bit of information out of this asshole that he could. The public location or the risk to himself meant nothing if Cat might be in trouble.

He and Hannibal parked their bikes next to the car. Max was half expecting him to take off, but the smug son of a bitch just smiled and rolled down his window. "Afternoon Brothers."

Max saw Hannibal grip his handles so hard the engine revved. "I'm not your Brother."

Out of time and patience, Max cut off whatever smart ass remark the man would have said. "Why are you following us, Pavel?"

The man shrugged and looked over at his dashboard before looking back. The smug look in his eyes bothered Max. "It is a nice day, and I was bored. Andrey heard you had gotten mixed up with the wrong sort of woman. I was curious."

The urge to pull his gun and threaten the man was like an itch that ran across his skin. When dealing with any of the criminal world it was a fine line they all had to walk to keep the peace. The knowledge that his woman might be in danger right now meant following those rules took a massive amount of control.

"Why do you care who I fuck, Pavel?" Max raised an eyebrow. "Oh man, you're jealous. Seriously, I'm flattered but I don't swing that way." Russian men were especially touchy about their sexuality. Pissing him off would be the fastest way without torture to get him to slip and tell them something.

Pavel opened his door and strode over. "Fuck you."

Max kicked down his Jiffy stand and swung off his bike. He closed the short distance so they were inches apart. Looking the over-muscled man up and down, he smirked.

"Like I said, not my thing, but I know some guys who would be happy to scratch that itch for you."

As expected, Pavel swung, and Max ducked. He punched the Russian right in the nerve cluster under the arm. The thug screamed and swung an elbow back. The guy wasn't a skilled fighter, probably used to his bulk being enough to win.

Max ducked and exchanged a few more blows, taunting the man with a face slap on the next pass. Pavel charged, and it was easy to trip him and wrap him up face down on the pavement in a submission hold.

"Tsk tsk, Pavel. Breaking the truce, attacking one of the Dark Sons." Neither Hawk nor Andrey would really consider this little scuffle a breaking of the truce, but taunting the man might get him more information. He moved so he had his knee in the Russian's back with the man's arm twisted behind him.

Pavel turned his face and spat. "You and your Club think you are such hot shit. Think you control Denver. Not for much longer. Your woman is dead and there isn't shit you can do about it."

Max jerked Pavel's arm and heard the satisfying pop as the man yelled. He wouldn't believe she was dead. Cat was a fighter. She could take care of herself. "So, you really are breaking the truce. You know damn well our women are off limits."

"Not officially yours." The Russian laughed, though he had to be in pain. "No patch, no protection. That house in the woods isn't claimed property. You and your Brothers can whine all you want like the mongrel dogs you are. Won't change that your bitch is dead."

His blood went cold. Max leaned down and whispered into Pavel's ear. "You had better hope that's not true because if she is, there is no treaty that will stop me from ending your life along with your boss and anyone else I think was responsible."

Max stood quickly and kicked the Russian in the head before he could respond. Pavel fell limp on the pavement. Not caring he was leaving an unconscious body in the parking lot, Max jumped on his bike.

Things weren't good if the Russians moved this openly against someone obviously connected to the Dark Sons. While the enforcer was right and they were within the letter of the agreement before, both sides held up the spirit as well.

Without a word to his Brother, he started the race back to Cat. He knew without a doubt that if anything had happened to his Wildcat, all the dark deeds in his past would look like a bright spring afternoon in comparison to what he would do to those responsible.

Chapter 21

You can run but you'll just die tired.

Avery scanned the unfamiliar property. How the hell was she going to face off against a five man hit team? Her life had devolved to the point that she believed she was in danger because this woman she just met said so.

Next to her, Akula grabbed a long bag that was attached to the side of her bike. She slung it over her shoulder with a practiced ease. The pat she gave to Avery's arm was probably supposed to be comforting. Unfortunately, the calculating glances left and right were a better indicator how much trouble they were in.

Strangely, for a house set back into the woods, the yard was cleared for about fifty yards in each direction. If they ran, they might make it into cover. Avery didn't like the odds if the car approaching saw them. They would be easy targets as the two of them ran across the equivalent of half a football field.

The house was large, but she didn't know the inside layout well enough to hide in or defend it. The building was only one story with a tower-like structure in the center of the roof. Cameras were at several positions along the edge of the roof. Avery chuckled. Well, at least Max would be able to find out what had happened to her if these men managed to kill her.

Akula looked up at one of the camera's and blew it a kiss. "I love snipers. Follow me."

The crazy Russian woman jogged along the edge of the house and jumped up. She appeared to snatch something out of the gutter. With a slight bang, a wood and rope ladder dropped to the ground. Akula climbed it like the thing was solid and securely bolted in place. Avery used the strap on the assault rifle to swing the weapon to her back, barely believing she was going to follow.

With a lot less grace, she climbed the ladder. In less than a minute, the two of them were walking across the sloping roof in a crouch. From their new vantage point, it was easy to see the tower-like outcropping was anything but decorative. It was made of cement with an iron ladder that gave access to a higher outlook configured suspiciously like a sniper tower.

Before Avery even understood what was going on, the woman had climbed up the ladder and was unpacking and assembling a rifle from her bag. By the time Avery reached the top, she could see a car as it pulled up to the house. Five men with assault rifles climbed out of the vehicle with determined looks on their faces. None of them noticed the two women. If there was any doubt these men meant harm, it was made obvious a few seconds later when they lined up and opened up on the house with automatic fire.

Akula bumped her shoulder with a laugh as she settled her gun on the edge of the bunker. "You just going to sit there?"

Avery settled her own gun, wincing as she heard glass shattering. Hannibal and Ink were not going to be happy their house got trashed. This was unreal. If she had been inside, God only knew what would have happened. She set her sights on the man closest to her, took a deep breath, and squeezed the trigger.

The sound of her rifle firing next to her ear without noise protection was painful, but she didn't let her aim falter as she moved to the next target.

The men had started to move, but before they could figure out where the shots were coming from, she pulled the trigger again and heard Akula's weapon bark next to her.

The one man still standing must have spotted them because he aimed up towards them. Avery ducked down behind the small wall and heard bullets slamming in from the other side. Between one breath and the next, everything was silent. She slowly turned and rose to look. All the men were motionless on the ground.

"Not bad, my friend, but I win." Avery swallowed and looked at the woman in disbelief. Calm, cool, and collected. There wasn't even a hint that Akula was bothered by the last few minutes. "I got three to your two. Also had to finish off your first one as he was still moving."

Avery's heart was beating in her throat, and her ears echoed from the loud noises. It was over so fast it didn't feel real. Akula smiled like they had finished a shooting game at a carnival. Here she was sitting in a sniper's perch, getting ribbed for not killing enough people. Her life was a mess.

"Are you going to tell me what the fuck is going on? How did you know what was going to happen?"

Akula shrugged. "Depends."

"On what?" Avery clenched her fists and fought back the urge to punch the person who had just saved her life.

"On if your man realized Viktor sent him into a trap." She was already packing up her weapon and scooping up her shells.

"Max and Hannibal are heading into a trap?" Avery gave the woman an angry glare. The thought of Max hurt because of her caused her throat to constrict. Damn it, every time she thought she had her feelings under control, something would happen to prove that she didn't.

"Not really." Akula stood and started climbing down the ladder at a quick pace.

"What the hell is that supposed to mean?" Avery followed the woman, not wanting her to get away before she had all her questions answered. If Max was in danger, she needed to head after them and see if they could help. This woman's motorcycle might be her only way to get to him.

"The trap was supposed to be me waiting on a roof to shoot them when they tried to get into Viktor's house. I am here. So they are safe."

Avery paused at the bottom of the ladder, trying to process what her new 'friend' had said. Max was safe. That was the important part. She took a deep breath as she watched Akula practically slide down the roof and on to the ground. She followed at a much slower pace, her body trembling as the adrenaline wore off.

"I thought you said Viktor was your enemy." She stood leaning against the house trying to get her body under control as Akula reattached her bag to the bike.

"No, what I said was I wanted him embarrassed then dead."

"How is that different from being his enemy?"

"We belong to the same family organization. It is complicated."

Translation, her savior was a member of the same Bratva as Victor. Why would Akula turn on her own organization?

Avery breathed through her nose and tried to remain calm. "So let me get this straight. You were supposed to kill Max and Hannibal when they came to Victor's house."

Akula smiled. "Yes."

"Instead, you came here to protect me."

"Yes."

Guess the woman wasn't in a sharing mood. None of this made sense to Avery. The urge to pull her hair and scream in frustration was building. This woman was obviously an assassin, but for some reason had protected her. It was hard not to be grateful. At the same time, she wanted to smack the shit out of the woman.

"So what now?" Avery was proud her tone was even.

Akula reached into her back pocket and pulled out a phone, and glanced down at it. Was the woman checking for messages? Now?

Whatever she saw must have pleased her, because Akula gave a small smile and nodded. She walked over to her bike and pulled the device she had used earlier to find the bug out of a side pouch. She walked back over to Avery.

"You need to use this to get the bug off your man, otherwise they will be following you everywhere. I don't think any of the other Brothers still have a tracking device on them. But you should warn them."

Avery looked down at the device. Shit, every moment that passed made her life feel more and more like a bad spy movie.

"Okay, and what do we do with the bodies?"

The Russian woman smiled. "I'm sure your man has a way to deal with them. I say you search them for anything that might be useful. Then when you talk to Hawk later, you'll need to tell him some things."

"What, you're not going to stick around to talk to your boyfriend?"

"He's not a boy, and he is so much more than a friend."

"I'm sure."

"Tell Hawk that he needs to not trust Andrey. Things are

happening in New York. And he needs to be vigilant. I will contact him later."

"And what about Victor?"

"If I were you I'd kill him because he won't stop until you are dead."

"I need him to clear my name and find out who really killed my partner."

"If you think there's any evidence left that could clear your name, you are a fool. And if you think he will tell you any information, you're doubly a fool."

"Then how am I supposed to prove my innocence?"

"That is not my problem." She threw her leg over her bike. "Meet me around front."

She kicked the motorcycle into gear. The sound loud. Avery gritted her teeth and stepped back, allowing the woman to turn the bike around.

Her thoughts were a jumble. Was this a hopeless situation? Was she going to have to remain on the run for the rest of her life? What kind of future was that? Hell, her future had already been confusing enough when she started having feelings for an outlaw biker. Would he be willing to stay with her if she was always on the run?

With her luck, it would be too much baggage, even for him. Akula pulled away, her bike speeding off down the road and Avery realized she wasn't going slow enough to stop at the front of the house. She started jogging and screamed for her to stop. But it was too late.

Avery surveyed the destruction of the house. The front was riddled with bullet holes, glass broken everywhere Her five attackers laid out like broken dolls in front of their car.

The crazy woman rode off down the road quickly, leaving the mess to her. Fuck, now what was she going to do?

Chapter 22

Relief: (Noun) That feeling when you almost piss yourself after a fucked-up situation.

Max could taste the adrenaline like acid on the back of his tongue. He swerved through traffic, racing to get back to Avery. Images of her lying dead flickered across his eyes as he tried to coax more speed out of his bike. He had already left Hannibal behind ten minutes ago.

He had left the highway cutting through shortcuts that would get him there much faster. Unfortunately, his Brother's bike wasn't customized for speed and off-road like Max's. It might have been smarter to stick together, but every second might mean the difference between life and death for Cat.

He rode through a dirt trail that bypassed almost five miles of twisting road, dodging trees and debris. He was only a minute or two away from the house when he raced onto the dirt driveway. He couldn't see the house yet, but he tried to prepare himself for whatever he would find.

It had been stupid not to question their orders. His Dark Sons Brothers weren't unreasonable. If he had taken five minutes to think, he would have realized Hawk would never have left a woman unguarded.

Racing through the last turn on the dirt road, the sight of an SUV parked in front of the house had his blood chilling. Max pulled a gun from his back, ready for anything. The motherfuckers were still here and would pay for any harm that had come to Cat tenfold.

Screw that. He would see them dead for even trying to hurt her. If he had been thinking straight, he would have stopped a little way down the road and snuck up on the place. But since surprise was no longer an option, he would have to act fast. Max raced past the car, gun extended and ready to fire. He would swing around the side of the home. If no one was back there, he would come in through the back.

Hopefully, his Wildcat had held out this long. There was no one standing between the car and the house. He braked hard and the bike almost skidded out from under him. Wrestling it under control, he stopped. Five men were sprawled out on the ground. From the blood splatter and gore, they were obviously dead.

"Wildcat!" he shouted over the noise of his own motorcycle.

What the fuck was going on? Were the attackers gone, only leaving the dead behind? Heart beating in his ears, he got off his bike. Gun at the ready if there was anyone still alive in the house.

Max looked around. The damage made his stomach drop. They had blown out every window on the front of the house. There were enough bullet holes in the walls that at least some of them had to make it through into the inside.

How could anyone have survived that?

"Max?"

The sound of Avery's voice sent a thrill through his system. She was alive! Max scanned the area, not seeing his Wildcat anywhere.

"Up here." Her laughter allowed the last of his tension to flow from his body. "Look up."

Max looked up and saw Cat sitting perched on what he had thought was a decorative steeple. She had an assault rifle slung across her body in an almost casual manner. In complete contradiction to the surroundings, she had a smile on her lips and a twinkle in her eye.

Max couldn't help but grin back. "I'm guessing they're all dead?" She nodded, and Max holstered his gun. "What made you think to go up there?"

He was amazed at her creativity. Just imagining the scene had his pulse jumping. The five men should have caught her unaware. How had she had the presence of mind to not only defend herself but take out five obviously well-armed attackers?

"Wasn't exactly my idea. Let me come down, and I'll explain it to you."

He watched as she scrambled down the back side of the roof. Max strode around the side of the house, needing to feel her in his arms. When she started down a rope ladder attached to the gutter of the house, Max couldn't wait any longer.

He grabbed her by the hips and spun her into his arms. It was awkward at first, as he had to push her rifle out of the way. No amount of oddness would stop him from feeling her body pressed against his.

Hugging her tight, Max inhaled her scent. Felt her breathing against his chest. It didn't matter how few days they had spent together, how little they knew of each other. Right now, here in this moment, he knew his life would never be the same without her in it.

She tilted her chin up and he took her mouth in a hungry kiss. The sweet taste of her was like a drug. For this woman, he would burn down the world.

Never again would he let anything come between them.

She pulled back slightly, and it took all his willpower to stop the kiss. "How did you know to come back here?" He loved how breathless her words were.

"We caught some idiot tailing us. With a little persuasion, he talked. Once we figured out that the whole thing was a trap, I raced to get back to you."

She chuckled, and he loved the sound. "There was supposed to be a sniper waiting for you at Victor's place. I'm glad you figured it out."

That the trap was for both of them surprised him. How the hell had someone set this up so quickly? Their enemies knew way too much. Had someone betrayed them? The idea that someone within the Dark Sons might have shared information had his gut roiling.

He leaned back and studied her face. "How do you know this? Did you manage to question some of the men who attacked you?"

A look of frustration flashed across Avery's face. "No, Hawk's girlfriend stopped by. She's quite a piece of work." Max felt her tremble under his hands. "She shared the plan. Victor apparently had some men slip some trackers on us at the motocross rally."

The thought he had grown so soft he hadn't noticed trackers was humbling. Confusion and anger swirled inside him. "Hawk doesn't have a girlfriend."

Cat shrugged. "She said it was complicated."

"No, I mean, he's never been with a woman for more than

a single night as far as I know." Who the hell was the woman who had come to warn Cat?

"Yeah, well, that's not what she said."

Max stepped back, his brain trying to process what could have happened. "You're telling me some woman showed up here claiming to be my President's girlfriend and you let her in? Then she warned you about the men that were coming. And what, took off?"

He didn't mean for his words to sound so suspicious, but he could tell by the flare of anger in her eyes that she wasn't happy with him. She stepped back and crossed her arms, putting more distance between them he didn't want.

"Yes, I'm telling you. That a badass chick showed up here. Claimed to be Hawk's booty call. Said she was an assassin hired to shoot you and Hannibal but didn't want to upset the big guy. Then she dragged me up to the roof, helped to take out five men sent here to kill me. Then took off on her bike." She pulled a black box out from her back pocket that looked like a bug sweeper. "Oh, and she gave me this."

Cat thrust the box into his chest while he tried to wrap his brain around what she had said.

Max step forward and cupped Cat's cheek. "I'm not doubting you, baby. This is a lot to take in."

She snorted, the sound too cute for the woman. "Tell me about it."

He held her face, wanting to lose himself in her gorgeous eyes. "I don't know what I would have done. If they'd killed you."

Max didn't like the look of guilt that filled his beautiful warrior's face. "Your life would be a lot easier if I wasn't in it."

"I don't want to hear that shit. I already told you, you're mine."

"Max. You can't keep saying things like that. You don't

know what's gonna happen. I might never be able to clear my name."

"You think I would give a shit about that?" He tipped her face up. "You are mine. If there's a way to clear your name, I'll find it. If there isn't, then who the fuck cares. But whatever we do, we'll do it together."

He didn't like the sight of tears shimmering in her eyes. But he knew his words were getting through to her.

"You really mean that, don't you?"

The sound of a motorcycle approaching at speed broke up their tender moment. Max grabbed Cat's hand and together they walked around to the front of the house to see Hannibal pull up. He parked next to Max's bike.

"Well damn. Is this your work, Max?" Hannibal gestured to the dead men then at the house.

Max shook his head. "Sorry about the house."

Hannibal ran a hand over the top of his skull. "Ink's gonna be pissed. But it looks like it's all fixable. Did you call Clean yet?"

"Not yet. I am still trying to figure out what went on here."

"What did go on here?" Hannibal looked over at the five dead men on the ground, then back at the house as if trying to recreate the action in his head. As an ex-sniper for The Rangers, Max thought he probably had the skills to figure it out. After a minute, the man smiled and looked over at Cat.

"Did you use my sniper perch?" The man didn't wait for an answer. He was intent on studying the bodies laid out on the ground "Some of these look like they were taken out with a high-powered rifle. Something I didn't leave with you."

Cat shrugged. "It's complicated. The short version is I had some help, but she's gone now."

"She?" Hannibal's raised eyebrow was a challenge, but Max was proud to see Cat didn't immediately lash out.

"Yeah, *she*. A woman named Akula said she was Hawk's

girlfriend. It's a long story. Do you guys think we should still be hanging out here?"

Max nodded. "You are right, Wildcat. Let me just send my Brother Clean a message and we'll get out of here. Then we need to figure out who this woman was and why she helped you."

Chapter 23

Life isn't fair. You aren't perfect. Accept those two truths and you'll be fucking golden.

The hour-long drive to a secret mountain cabin gave Avery way too much time to think. Akula's words played over in her mind, eroding her confidence. What if there wasn't any evidence to prove her innocence? And if there wasn't, what was she going to do?

A lifetime spent on the run would be a nightmare. Having to change her name, always wondering when she would be caught, and never being safe was a reality she didn't want to live. But going back to jail, having to dodge assassins for the rest of her life, however short it would be, was even worse.

She'd never been the type of person to give up the fight, no matter how hard. Nate had been her only friend, and he'd paid for that mistake with his life. She needed not only to find the person who killed her partner but also to make them pay. Avery owed him that much.

She also needed to take Victor down. Leaving a snake in the grass like him free wasn't acceptable. The amount of damage he could do in his position to other innocent people was unfathomable. But would anyone believe her? Even if she proved she didn't commit the crimes she was accused of, the taint of doubt would always be there. Who would ever trust her again?

The temptation to walk away was almost overwhelming. She could ride off into the sunset with Max and start over. Now, wasn't that a crazy idea? Her dreams had definitely changed over the last year.

She had never wanted the usual fantasy of a house with a white picket fence. Hell, she hadn't even dreamed the more modern ideal of being part of a power couple who lived in a high-rise condo. All she had ever wanted was to make a difference in the world. To be part of what made this country safe for those with idealistic dreams.

Now that was all gone. What small amount of faith she'd held in the system was shattered. The world was a fucked up place. Good and bad were only black and white when you were a child. The grown up world contained nothing but shades of gray. These thoughts were a waste of time.

The only thing she could hope for was the closure of finding out the truth. It was a simple plan. Find out who killed her partner, and expose Victor. It wouldn't be easy, but even if it meant giving up her own life, she would find a way.

Avery was so lost in her thoughts, she hadn't noticed they had reached their destination until the motorcycle shut off. Deep in the woods of the mountains, she had no clue as to their location in relation to any sort of civilization. Max had parked them in front of something that she might generously call a shack.

The one story wooden building was barely big enough to be called a house. Everything about the place screamed, crazy mountain man. She had never believed she was a city girl until now. The thought that the place might be infested with all sorts of wild animals or bugs made her skin crawl. Was there even enough room in that place for an inside bathroom?

After sitting for a few seconds, the bike turned off, and she knew it was time to move. Her muscles screamed in protest as she swung off and tried to get her balance on the forest floor. She had never really realized how many muscles it took to ride on the back of a motorcycle.

Her back popped as she stretched. "You take me to the nicest places."

Max chuckled and swung off the bike with obnoxious ease, not showing a single sign of discomfort. "Well, it isn't luxury. But I promise no one's gonna find us here."

Avery winced. It wasn't that she had forgotten why they were here, more that she wanted to forget. Maybe she was getting too used to being safe around Max. He had insisted they sweep everything they had for bugs before even taking off to find this place.

After finding the tracker on his bike, Max had insisted on re-sweeping everything. Avery lost her patience the third time he made her stand still for a search and ended up getting a hard swat on her ass for her bitching. The idea that he cared so much about her was foreign, so his heightened sense of overprotectiveness felt a little overwhelming.

"How long are we going to be here?" She stepped to the left and saw a fairly new black pickup truck parked alongside the cabin. Did somebody actually live here?

"Hawk's gonna be joining us later. He wasn't able to give me much information, so he's going to be bringing information and supplies."

"So, a long time?" It was hard not to tease him when he got all serious.

"Once we make a plan, I'll inform you of what it is."

Max's expression didn't change, her teasing having little to no outward effect.

"Yes, Sir, Mountain Sergeant Sir." Avery flicked him a salute. "The little lady will stay quiet and enjoy her camping."

Max's stoic expression broke into a smile, and he barked a startled laugh. Avery loved the sound of it and smiled back at him. She took perverse pleasure in the fact she could make him happy.

"This isn't camping. This is nothing but the best for my delicate lady."

Avery resisted the urge to stick out her tongue. "Thanks, I'm overwhelmed with the luxury."

Max's smile faded. "It really is compared to some places I've stayed. I can't tell you how many times I've slept out without a roof over my head."

Her curiosity was piqued. "Was that back during your time in the military?"

Would he share something from his past? He had opened up to her before, but it seemed like a rare occurrence. Everything she had learned about him made her want to discover more. Her feelings for him grew with everything she learned. She still felt like she had barely scratched the surface of the complicated man.

"I haven't had to do anything as rough as the men stationed in the desert." He looked up at the night sky. "My missions were more in Eastern European countries or China. But there were a few times on my way to or from a mission that there wasn't any sort of lodging available. So I did what was necessary."

Max strode away without a glance, up the two steps, across the wooden porch and through the open door to the cabin. She could tell he was uncomfortable. But she wasn't ready to give up on their conversation just yet.

Avery followed him inside and found the cabin had a

studio apartment layout. One large room with some appliances against the back wall. A bed was against the left wall and a single door that probably led, thank goodness, to the bathroom off to the right. She came up behind her gorgeous man and wrapped her arms around his waist.

"Why did you leave the military?"

"Not sure you'd actually say I left. More, I'd done my time." He turned around, wrapped his arms around her. "The service I was in, there isn't any leaving. Or at least not in the conventional sense."

"What do you mean?"

"I mean, I knew things and did things, that Uncle Sam never wanted the general populace to know about. I always knew the only way out was in a pine box." His grip tightened a bit, and her heart skipped a beat.

"But you're out. And you're here." Or was he still in? What was he trying to tell her?

"Yeah, but Uncle Sam doesn't know that."

"What do you mean?"

"I mean, when I finally realized I couldn't follow their orders anymore. Wouldn't do the things they asked me to do. I made a choice." He stroked her hair, as if trying to gain comfort from the touch.

"What did they want you to do?" She held her breath, trying to picture what could be so bad to make a man who had obviously been dedicated to service, question that service.

"They wanted me to take out a man by blowing up the building he was in." Max's voice was tight, as if he was having to force out the words.

She pressed her cheek against his chest, wanting to give comfort, but needing to know his story. "I'm assuming this wasn't a good man."

"No, he was a terrorist leader. Had a list of crimes he was responsible for that would horrify anyone to read them."

"So what was the problem?" She somehow knew it wasn't the killing that had made him blink.

"His family and the families of his followers were all in that building. Women, children, over thirty innocent lives who would die with him if the building blew. Their only crime being married to or related to the scum of the Earth." He took a shuddering breath. "Most of them had been as abused as you hear in any horror story."

"Oh, my God. Why would they want you to blow up the building then? Couldn't you take only him out?" She knew collateral damage was often a very real part of any military action, but the numbers seemed to be too high for even the coldest of hearts to find acceptable.

"No, the piece of shit never left the inner compound." Avery could almost feel the frustration vibrating through his chest. "I scouted that place for over a month to look for an opportunity to take him out. He was too smart to show his head where a sniper bullet might hit it. No one but his inner circle ever got to see him. It would have taken years to work my way in to seeing him face to face. We had no agents anywhere even close to his inner circle."

"They didn't think it was worth the wait?"

"No. So I suggested a strike team. The place was well fortified, so we still might take out some innocents. But at least that way we could save as many as possible. Not blow up children in their beds."

"I'm guessing your superiors didn't like that idea." Avery's heart ached for the obvious pain contained within his words.

His chuckle held no humor. "Nope. The brainiacs in command all assessed there was too much of a risk he might escape during a firefight."

"So what did you do?" She didn't want to believe he would have gone through with it. That would have haunted colder men than him.

"I got command to agree to station strike teams at all the known exits to the compound. Used the excuse they might have fortified some of the rooms and didn't want to risk him escaping. Then I went in with the explosives."

Her throat closed up. Was there really any good excuse for forcing someone to kill like that? The impossible choice forced onto a soldier was cruel. To leave a man alive to do horrible crimes or to kill innocents and turn yourself into something evil. The excuse of the greater good had to be cold comfort when the cries of children would haunt your dreams.

"Did you get him?"

Max leaned down and kissed her cheek. "Not exactly. But he did die that night." There was a sense of satisfaction in his voice that gave her hope.

"What did you do?"

"The reports all say there was a fault in the trigger on the explosives I was carrying. They went off before I could get them into position. Instead of taking down the building, they took out a guard shack on the edge of the camp. To anyone watching, the explosion ended the career and life of an unnamed Black Ops agent. However, the bombs sent the rats scurrying, racing out all the exits. A sniper team was able to take out the target along with most of his inner circle." This time his chuckle held a little warmth. "I got several post-humous decorations since, even though I had been incompetent enough to get myself blown up, my planning meant the mission was still a success."

"So they believe you're dead." The giggle she gave was both at the ridiculousness of the situation and a release of stress.

"Oh, absolutely. If anyone in the blacker parts of the government ever found out I was alive, I wouldn't remain that way for much longer."

"That has to be stressful." His situation was more like hers than she had known. Though having people believe he was dead was probably easier than being actively hunted. But one slip could change that.

"Not really. People don't look for dead people. My current identity is solid, but even if it wasn't, while I won't be stupid, I refuse to live my life worrying about what might happen."

"How did you end up with the Dark Sons?" Going from one side of the law to the other had to be an interesting story. Hopefully, one that would lighten the mood.

"I bought a motorcycle. I was riding around trying to figure out what I was gonna do with my life." His grip around her loosened, and she leaned back and gave him a smile. "It was a crazy feeling. I had never really had that freedom before. There was a mission early in my career and several of the men on the SEAL Team were members of the Dark Sons, Los Angeles. Hell, I barely remembered them or the mission, but I ran into them at a bar. When they recognized me, I should have pretended not to know them but I needed to connect with some other human beings for a while."

She smiled and enjoyed how the memory seemed to light up his eyes. "So they didn't turn you in?"

"No. Though they only knew one of my many cover names and none of what had gone on. They accepted me, no questions asked. Offered me a brotherhood. One the military had denied me when they pulled me out of the Marines in boot camp. I never regretted it. They don't care who I was, only who I am now. They will have my back no matter what."

Avery closed her eyes and leaned against his broad chest. What would it be like to really belong somewhere? Have people willing to have your back no matter what. She had never had anything like that in her life. The feel of Max's arms around her was the most comfort anyone had offered her since childhood.

"I'm worried Akula might have been right." It was easier

to speak the words when she wasn't looking at him and with the warmth of his chest pressed up against her cheek. "What if there is no way to prove myself innocent?"

"Then we figure something else out." It was such a simple sentence that gave her more hope when spoken by someone else.

"Victor has to pay." Max needed to understand that while she might give up on proving herself innocent, she would not give up on vengeance for Nate.

"Don't worry about that, Wildcat. I let him go once. That won't be happening again." The feeling of him kissing the top of her head made her smile. "Either way, there's nothing we can do right now. It's been a long day and we're both exhausted."

"We should try to grab some sleep before Hawk gets here."

"How long do you think he'll be?"

"He's at least going to be another hour or two. I'll get a message when he's on his way. And from that point, we're still another hour out from where he is right now." She knew they should probably move, but she was going to stay in his arms as long as he let her.

"What did he say about Akula?"

"He didn't say much. But I don't think he could talk freely."

"Do you think she is his girlfriend?" Avery's head bounced up and down as Max chuckled.

"Who knows? That man might even have more mysteries than I do." Max took a deep breath. "I don't think she gave you her real name."

"Why not?"

"Akula isn't a common name, but it means shark in Russian. If she's what I suspect she is, it is probably a reference to a type of blade used in hunting."

"Well, I guess it shouldn't surprise me. Since none of you like to use real names."

"What, you don't like your new name, Wildcat?"

Avery shrugged. They stood like that for a few minutes, and she let the silence and the warmth of his arms help her mind drift. If she didn't clear her name, she would have to adopt a new one. If she was honest with herself, she really enjoyed the Wildcat nickname Max had given her. It was another one of those things that showed he didn't think she was weak. Could she think of herself that way?

Maybe it was time to start owning her new identity. Changing who she was. It didn't mean giving up her past goals, just making new ones. The truth was, she would need to redefine herself, even if she managed to prove her innocence. She would start over. Do something she wanted. How much more blood would she have on her hands before she would be free to start fresh?

Chapter 24

It's not the skeletons in a person's closet you have to worry about. It's the zombies.

Max enjoyed the warm feeling of his woman sleeping against his chest. She was exhausted and probably needed more than a single night of good sleep. The minute they had lain down, she had lost consciousness. It was humbling the amount of trust that showed.

Victor was a snake in the grass, and Max had no problem eliminating him. But would taking him out solve her problems? She needed closure more than anything else. Cat deserved to live in the light instead of in the shadows with him.

The truth of the matter was, he was a selfish man. He didn't want to give her up. Confronting Victor without killing him risked exposure. If the Russians discovered he was still alive, they would want him dead. But that wasn't what worried him.

If people within the Bratva connected him to his old identity, then it was very probable that Uncle Sam would find out he wasn't dead as well. Faking his own death was probably something that could only be done once. But if it was a choice between getting Wildcat what she needed and exposing himself, he would take that risk.

The sound of the motorcycle coming closer to the cabin wasn't a surprise, since he had received a text from Hawk about an hour ago. Max slipped his arm out from underneath Cat's head and gave a small smile as she grumbled and crawled deeper into the blankets. She would be pissed at him later if he didn't wake her, but she needed her sleep and he needed some time to talk to his President.

Max walked out into the evening to wait on the porch, closing the door behind him. The night air was slightly cool, but not so cold he needed a jacket. All around him the night animals went silent as the rumble of a bike echoed through the night, as it approached. Hopefully, the sound wouldn't wake Cat.

The noise cut off, leaving only the echoing silence of a mountain night. Hawk pulled some bags off his bike and joined him on the porch with a serious expression that told Max he didn't have good news.

"Hey, Brother, good to see you." They clasped forearms. Hawk dropped the bags on the ground before sitting down.

Max wished he had a beer, but they had discovered earlier supplies at the cabin were very limited. Water and canned goods. Hopefully, those bags his President had just dropped contained more than clothes. Otherwise, if they were going to be staying here for more than a day, he would have to get supplies.

Ending his mental stalling, Max asked, "Any fallout from the police raids?"

His President shook his head. "Their warrants were specific to searching for your woman so they didn't get to poke around too much." Hawk reached into one of the bags and pulled out two beers. He handed one over, then opened his and took a sip. "After they brought in the dogs, they tore apart your place and the basement of the Clubhouse."

Max didn't like the fact that anyone had been in his house. He didn't keep anything illegal there, so it wouldn't be a problem, but it still grated on his nerves. "I'm surprised he pushed the whole thing as far as he did since we know the whole raid was a setup to flush us out for the assassins."

"This is a dangerous thing that we've gotten pulled into the middle of. Victor Taylor is considered by the US government to be a legitimate FBI agent. If what you said it true, he's a double agent." Hawk took a long pull from his beer. "According to Tek's search, he was born in Wisconsin. Went to college here in the States, top of his class and all that shit. Recruited into the FBI on graduation. And he's had a stellar career, completely free of any funny business."

Max frowned. "I know that isn't true. There is no mistake. He might have one of the best covers I've ever seen, but that fucker is Viktor. A sadist and sick son of a bitch who enjoys making people scream before they die. I can't believe he is even able to fake legit well enough to stay out of trouble for a few months, never mind the years he has to have been doing it."

"That's where things get interesting. The only reason Cami could break his cover is because of the photos from your file. There is nothing digital tracing these two people to each other. According to the records Viktor Gunav was murdered in New York five years ago, at the same time Victor Taylor was transferred to Colorado. Covers like that aren't easy or cheap to establish."

"I know." It was hard to understand why they would have taken this risk or gone to this expense for a man like Viktor.

"You should have told me you had an unpleasant history with the Stepanov Bratva." Hawk leaned forward, his mouth tight with displeasure.

"I was barely a low level soldier with the Borisyuk Clan over in Russia while they were still in thick with the KGB. My cover was never blown, and I never thought any of the people who I knew would come over to the US."

"That clan got absorbed into the Stepanov Bratva and most of them were sent to New York to expand. What happens if they find out you are alive?"

Max leaned back and took a long drink from his beer. "With them? They'll assume I was a traitor of some sort and probably want me dead. If they start digging into my old cover than it will probably set off alarms here in the US that would make my life very difficult."

Hawk nodded. It wasn't a secret to him that Max had faked his death to get out of Black Ops, even if the details weren't openly shared.

"The men at Hannibal and Ink's house were Russian, a hit squad flown in from New York. Best guess is they don't want his cover blown so Viktor has back up from Andrey Petrov locally as well as anything he can get from both in and out of the country."

"And your girlfriend?" For the first time in his life, Max saw his President hesitate.

Hawk took a visible breath and leaned back in his chair. "She's someone I know. Someone I've known a long time."

"But is she your girl?" Max watched as hundreds of tiny expressions flickered across his President's face.

"No." Only years of practice let him hide his shock as he

realized the man he trusted to the core of his existence had just lied to him. If it had been any other person, he would have called him on it. Why would he lie about something as insignificant as a lover? Unless she was more to him than that.

Their relationship wasn't of importance in the here and now. Hawk had earned his privacy, so he would let it go. For now.

"Okay. What is she then?"

"She's a Bratva assassin who would do anything her family tells her to."

If anyone else had been listening to the man, they might have believed that this woman meant nothing to him. But Max could see the tightness around his eyes, brief twitches along his jaw that spoke of deep emotion. What had this woman done to his friend?

"Why is she helping us, then?"

"I've helped her out a few times. Maybe she thinks this will pay me back." There was no doubt in Max's mind that Hawk didn't think it was nearly enough.

"Is she trustworthy?"

Hawk rubbed a hand over his face. "In this case, I think she is. For the last few years, there has been chatter about movement within the Bratva families. Especially hers. I don't know exactly what's going on there, but my guess is she's in the middle of it somehow."

"She said she'd contact you."

"Yeah, I got a text from a burner phone. Said to meet her tomorrow night at our usual bonfire spot up on the mountain. She wants both of you there, or she won't deliver."

That spot was used to meet with people they didn't trust within the compound or for parties with clubs who might not respect their rules. It wasn't exactly a secret, but it also wasn't common knowledge. "Do you think it's a trap?"

"Anything's possible with her." The exhaustion in those words spoke of years of disappointment and frustration.

"Are we going to meet her?"

"Considering both of our resident geniuses can't get shit on this guy digitally. If we want the information, I don't see that we have much choice. Would your woman be willing to disappear, start over somewhere else? That would be a much simpler solution."

"No. Bringing this asshole to justice means much too much to her. Hell, it means too much to me. I let this asshole go once because Uncle Sam ordered me to. Now I find out he's infiltrated our government and done God knows what with that information." Max shook his head. "No, I can't let it go."

Hawk nodded his head towards the cabin door. "You going to claim her?"

Max nodded, the decision solidifying in his mind. Almost from the moment he saw her again they had been racing towards that outcome. Logic be damned. This woman was his.

"Good. We're in an awkward spot right now. Technically, the Bratva had a hit on her before you came into the picture. If they do anything to her, even after you claim her, I'm not sure what National will do."

"Are you saying they wouldn't back my claim?" Brotherhood was supposed to mean having someone at your back no matter how hard the situation. The idea that they wouldn't be there was like a cold splash of water.

"No, I'm just saying this is really complicated and will cause all of us possibly fatal headaches. If you don't have a claim on her, there's no way National would back us if we decided to go to war. With the claim they won't be happy but they will be there. Brothers and their families first. Friends and outsiders are a distant second and that includes treaties."

He hated he might put them all at risk, but she was worth it. Brotherhood had always been enough for him to give all his loyalty to the Dark Sons. Over the last year, he had seen some of his Brothers find their women and wondered why they had been willing to risk it all for them. Now he understood.

"Do you think there's a chance the Bratva will back off if I claim her? I might be able to convince her to let revenge go if it would mean not having a price on her head."

"No. Though that is probably for the best, because I doubt you could convince your woman to back down. From what I understand, this is now a pride thing for the Russians. They said she must die, so she must die. All of them have too much fucking pride." Max was surprised by the amount of venom in Hawk's last statement.

That was it. Tomorrow night, they would get the information they needed to bring Victor down or end up at war with the Russians.

Chapter 25

If you know what you want, don't settle. Grab your happiness by the balls and make it your bitch.

Avery sat on a log and pretended to drink her beer. The bark of her makeshift chair bit into the back of her too bare thighs. She was uncomfortable, to say the least, dressed in skimpy borrowed clothes, warmed by a bonfire, and surrounded by men putting themselves at risk for her. She did her best to look confident. Pretending anxiety and fear weren't tearing through her stomach like two opposing tornadoes wasn't easy.

She tilted her head back and tried to find some calm. She focused on the night sky. In the mountains, it was an endless field of stars that could only be seen once you got away from the city. The day in the cabin had been like a serene pocket of time where none of her problems existed. Max had woken her up with a gigantic breakfast made with supplies Hawk had brought in while she had slept. It had been tempting to get angry about not being woken, but even she had to admit she had needed the sleep.

After eating, the two of them had walked in the woods. For the first time in her life, she'd shared with someone the funnier stories from her years in foster care. He told her tales of when he had been a crazy, reckless boy. Who would have thought that she could do sweet? But those couple of hours when it was only the two of them, that's what it had been. Unfortunately, all good things come to an end.

Now they were sitting at a remote location with about twenty of his Brothers waiting for a crazy Russian woman to bring them information. Or they might be waiting for an ambush. From the visible weapons on the men around her, she figured they were ready for either. Not that they had given her a gun. It was hard trusting these strangers with her safety, but she didn't have much choice.

It's not that she didn't like his Brothers. Most of them seemed nice. She chuckled to herself. It was hard to believe that she was calling a bunch of outlaw bikers nice. Things had changed so much in her life. It was easy to see how much Max cared for all of these people, how close he was to each one of them. Unlike her, all of them appeared relaxed but alert.

A vibration in her pocket startled her. She put her beer down on the ground and dug into her pocket for the small satellite phone Max had given her earlier. Who the heck would be calling her? Max was sitting and chatting with several of his brothers closer to the fire. Avery looked at the display across it in block letters were the words *The Great and Powerful Ozena.*

Confused, she hit the talk button. "Hello?"

"Hey spy lady!" Avery recognized Cami's voice.

Of course it would be her. "What's up?"

"Just checking in on you. The boys wouldn't let us come no matter how much we begged."

Avery laughed. "You call them boys to their faces?"

"Only when they d-don't do what I want." It was impressive how the woman was capable of pouting even over the phone.

"It was probably smart of them. Who knows what Akula has planned? How much do you know about what's going on here tonight?" Avery could almost picture Cami making a face.

"I know a lot more than they want me to. But a lot less than I'd like to." Cami giggled. "See, that was spectacularly vague. I'm thinking if I get my spy craft down right maybe they'll let me in on more *Club Business.*"

Avery doubted it. In her experience, men rarely shared more than they thought was necessary. But there was no reason to burst the woman's bubble. "Let me know how that works out for you. So why did you call?" She wasn't trying to be rude, but the truth was they didn't have a close relationship and she had never gotten a phone call that was for the sole purpose of chatting. Truth was she didn't know these women well enough to understand why they did anything they did.

Max looked over at her, and she enjoyed the smile that tipped up his lips. His expression blanked as he walked towards her.

"I wanted to find out if anything had happened yet."

"No. I don't think anything is supposed to happen for another hour or so." Avery bit her lip, not sure if she should be sharing that much.

"Oh, I don't mean that. I mean, has anything else happened?"

"Did he ask her yet?" Pixie shouted in the background.

Max came closer and gave her a puzzled look. "Who's on the phone?"

Avery held up a finger. "Did he ask me what yet?" She

covered the phone and mouthed Cami and hoped he was able to read her lips.

Max raised an eyebrow. Clearly not happy. Was it what she just said or who she was talking to that bothered him?

"Nothing. I didn't s-say anything about anyone asking yo-you anything." Cami's voice betrayed her nerves. "Pixie was the one who s-said something, remember that."

These women were absolutely nuts. "Okay. Then ask Pixie who is supposed to be asking me what."

Max's lips tightened, and he reached forward, snatching the phone out of her hand. "Goodbye, ladies."

Much to her annoyance, he pressed the end button, cutting off the conversation. She gritted her teeth, trying not to growl. "Did I say you could end my conversation?"

"No. But this phone is supposed to be for emergencies only. Was what she was talking to you about an emergency?"

"I don't know. Since you didn't let her finish telling me." It probably wasn't, but it wasn't like she had called them, so she didn't appreciate his lecturing tone.

Max sighed and reached out his hand to help her up. She considered giving him an attitude. In fact, it was almost a physical need to do so to prove she didn't need his help. Avery took a deep breath. She was trying to let him in and that would never happen if she didn't start letting down her defenses. She took his hand, and he pulled her up. His warm eyes looked down at her and the bonfire light reflected in their dark depths.

"That was just Old Ladies being nosy and trying to ruin something I planned to surprise you with tonight." The warm feeling of his arms wrapped around her made her feel safe.

None of them could predict what was going to happen tonight. Akula might walk into the camp, hand them the information, and leave. Or gunmen could drop from the sky to kill them all. The fact that so many of his Brothers were willing to risk any potential danger, for her, was almost overwhelming.

It was simple for them. Max had asked, and they were there. Somehow in the middle of that, he had planned something. "So you've got a surprise for me?"

"I don't know if I'd call it a surprise, really. But I do have something to ask you." His hand gently brushed the hair away from her face and heat rose to Avery's cheeks. "Wildcat, I want you to be my Old Lady. I will warn you— it's a commitment, for all time. But you will also have protection and a family for life. Will you stand by me and my Brothers no matter how hard the test, no matter how big the challenge, or how dangerous the fight?" Avery barely noticed how Max's voice had raised as he asked her the questions and how quiet the murmurings of his Brothers' conversations had become.

His words shocked her, and her heart thudded in her throat. "This is forever for you, isn't it?" Max nodded.

She loved him. Had admitted it to herself only yesterday, but never dreamed he would return her feelings. Why he wanted to be part of her crazy life and take on all the problems that entailed, she didn't understand. But his love, this strange family he belonged to, that was something she wanted more than anything else in the world.

"Yes, Max. As crazy as it is. As fast as this has happened. I want to be yours. I want you to be mine."

"You're mine now and forever." He cupped her cheek. "Dark Sons for life." Max's voice was a growl that echoed in the silent night. She rose up on her tiptoes and nipped his lip with a soft growl.

"Dark Sons for life." All the Brothers present echoed his words as his mouth crashed down on hers in a kiss that stole her breath.

Heat rose in her core. She wanted this man inside her forever and always. Not just inside her body, but inside her heart and soul. When the women had first described what claiming her as an Old Lady would entail. She had thought it barbaric, a macho exercise that she wanted nothing to do with.

Now, in that moment, she understood. It wasn't about public sex or satisfying some sort of kinky ritual. It was about declaring they were one in a way that went beyond the civilized constraints of society. Throwing off all expectations and limitations and claiming one another.

He pulled back, and she couldn't help the moan that escaped her lips. She clutched onto his shirt, not wanting even an inch of space between them. His gentle kiss on her forehead was sweet. Wait a minute. What the hell was that? She didn't want gentle or sweet.

Fire built inside her and she saw the same passion echoed in his eyes. But his face was a picture of locked down control. Why was he holding back? It was hard to think more than *want more now* but she somehow managed to focus.

"I thought this is the part where you claim me." Her skin was alive, craving his touch.

His eyes seemed to spark. "I did claim you."

"Okay, but I mean…" He brushed her face with a gentle caress, and that made her angry. Why wasn't he acting the way she expected? "I thought you had to fuck me." Her words were a snarl.

He stepped forward, and she moved back as he stalked closer. The desire of his body was a tangible force between them. Their steps had moved them from the center of the gathering to the edge. Everyone's attention was on them, and she didn't care.

"No, I don't *have* to fuck you, Wildcat." His words shivered down her skin, and her nipples tightened painfully.

"That's not what the Old Ladies said." She lifted her chin

in challenge. A few chuckles could be heard. But the night was dim, and it was impossible to tell who they came from.

"Is that what you want? While we're sitting here waiting for a possible enemy. You want me to shove up that, way too short, skirt. Force you down on the ground. Fuck you till you're screaming my name."

She clenched her fists in frustration. His words turned her on, making her core ache, but they also annoyed her. Was it selfish for her to want him to want her, no matter the situation? He had started this. She didn't care about the danger. Besides, with all of his Brothers around wouldn't they be safe?

Foolish or not, she needed him inside her. Claiming her so she would know, without a shadow of a doubt, that he was never going to leave her. Anger won control of her mouth and she lashed out. "It's okay if you can't get it up under the circumstances. I completely understand."

Her words were a challenge. She might be trying to rein in her natural tendency to lash out when angry or frustrated, but the truth was, this is who she was. This was who he knew she was. He had proven that he didn't care. He liked her fire. So she was going to let him see it. Make him understand that his hesitation hurt her.

Max grabbed her wrist and placed her hand against his crotch. He was hard, his thick length straining against his jeans. Her nipples pulsed with pleasure, and her excitement dripped down her inner thigh. When she had found the bag of clothing at the edge of the bed this morning, she'd been a little annoyed that the only options for clothes were this short jean skirt and the lightweight scoop neck t-shirt. Now she was glad for it. Nothing would be in the way if she could get him to act on the desire she saw burning in his gaze.

"Does this feel like I don't want you?"

"Well, it does seem like you're a little excited." His growl sparked something inside her.

Pain and excitement raced down her spine as he gripped her hair and forced her head back.

"Little." He chuckled. "Well, I guess we're going to have to fuck that sass right out of you. Show every one of my Brothers you're mine in every way."

He held her so she couldn't see anything but him. She felt the gazes of some of the Brothers on her skin. Avery didn't care. She needed this man, needed him in a way that defied all logic or reason. Needed him to make her his.

Chapter 26

Having friends in low places means that even while going through hell you will have someone at your back.

Normally in a situation that might be dangerous, Max wouldn't have let Cat get her way. But while he had ten of his brothers visible around him, there were another fifteen hidden in the woods and monitored cameras along the road. That meant they would have plenty of warning before Akula arrived.

"Claim your woman we have your back." Max heard Hawk chuckle through his bone conduction earpiece.

That knowledge and his President's words were all the permission he needed to give her what she needed. Sex in front of an audience didn't bother him. He had watched as his brothers claimed their women, understood the primal message of it all.

Cat was right. They both needed this. Needed to declare themselves in more than words in front of everyone.

"Hands on the log." He let go of her hair and enjoyed the way she swayed.

Her eyes flared with desire, then she moved with a sexy grace. The few steps she took were a test of his will as he traced every curve of her body with his eyes. Her tiny smile told him he was about to get a surprise.

The log he had indicated was large, but she still had to bend over at the waist, so her ass was pointing right towards him. Max enjoyed the way the fabric of her skirt slid up her thighs, till it revealed her bare ass underneath. Fuck, if he had known she wasn't wearing underwear this entire time, his concentration would have been shit. He stepped forward and enjoyed the smooth feel of her skin against his palms as he ran his hands up the backs of her thighs.

"Why the hell aren't you wearing any underwear?" He didn't bother to hide the hunger in his voice.

"There wasn't any in the bag you left me."

Max chuckled and smacked her ass at her saucy reply. If one of his brothers had packed the bag, he would have believed it was an oversight. But he knew the Old Ladies had packed for her. Instead of sensible clothes. They had dressed her up to seduce him.

He would have to thank them for it later. His fingers played across her gorgeous tempting crease. Her honey was visible even in the dim light. Her moan as his finger slid through her folds and found the little pearl of pleasure made his cock pulse. Cat's sounds weren't loud enough. If he was going do this, he was going do it right.

He used his other hand to slap her ass, enjoying the sound of flesh hitting flesh. "You wanted this, Wildcat. Don't hide your sounds from me."

She pushed back against him with a little wiggle. "You have to give me something to make noise about."

God, he loved her sass. Everything about her challenged

him in the best possible way. She was wild, surprising, and rarely did what he expected. No moment with this woman would ever be boring.

He circled her clit with one hand while peppering down blows on either side of her ass. Cat's pants and moans were music in the evening as her breath started to catch. He thrust two fingers deep into her core. Her scream of pleasure was music to his ears.

It only took a few pumps, and she was trembling against his hand. He wanted to draw this out, push her to the point she begged for him, but the temptation of her and the needs of his own body were too great.

He undid his pants and the pleasure of freeing his cock from the tight confines of his jeans forced a groan from him. Max gripped her hips and pulled her into position. The sight of his fingers as they pressed into her flesh was amazing. Her whimper begged for him to take her. They were made for one another, their needs perfectly aligned.

Max thrust forward, and her body welcomed him. Cat's tight muscles clenched around his length like a vise. This was where he belonged. This was his home.

She tried to buck against him, but he held her still, needing to savor the moment. He enjoyed knowing she would have bruises where his fingers gripped her so tightly. A mark to remind her she was his. He reached forward and wrapped her hair around his hand, forcing her body to arch up beautifully.

"You're mine," he growled.

"Yes!" Her response was a shout as she tried to thrash against him.

Only then did he release his tightly coiled control and set the rhythm that both her body and his needed. They were in perfect synchronization. He didn't even bother to try to hold back his own sounds of pleasure.

Every thrust brought him to the ends of her depths, and

he marveled at how perfectly their bodies fit. It was like she had been created for him so that they were able to lose themselves in the most primal of rhythms.

Her body, her soul, her spirit. All of it was the perfect match for his own. When she started to tighten around him his own orgasm built in his spine.

"I love you, Wildcat."

"Oh God, I love you, Max." Her words were a scream that probably was heard for miles.

Her body spasmed and milked his orgasm straight out of his body. Lightning jolts of pleasure raced across his skin then seemed to flow into her body and back to him.

Silence fell, only the popping of the bonfire making any sound other than their harsh breathing. He finally forced himself to pull out of her. The sight of his cum dripping out of her and down her leg was probably the sexiest thing he had ever seen.

He pulled her up, and turned her so her body pressed against his. Max needed to hold her against him for a minute. Their heartbeats thundered against each other's chests. Over her head, he caught Hawk's eye, and the man gave him a smile and a chin lift.

Max wasn't sure how long they had stood there holding each other but eventually the moment was broken by a crackle over his earpiece.

"Drone incoming," Dragon spoke.

What the hell? He stepped back and pulled Avery behind him. There was a big tree close to them, so he maneuvered her so the tree was at her back.

"Stay behind me." Max hoped she wouldn't resist him.

"What's going on?" Her voice was calm, and he was glad to hear it lacked fear.

"I'm not sure—"

"Drone doesn't have any obvious weapons. It is carrying a

small thin package." Dragon's voice cut him off.

"Heads up, everyone. This could be a distraction." Hawk's voice echoed through the clearing.

"Dragon spotted a drone," Max whispered. Damn it, he should have gotten her an earpiece so she would know what was going on. If the shit hit the fan, she would be completely dependent on him. A tense minute passed before Max finally heard the unmistakable sound of a mechanized drone.

When Max could make out the shape of the flying object, he could see it was a small, commercially available model that was carrying something that looked like a manila envelope. The drone flew over their heads and hovered above Hawk before dropping the object. The scowl on his President's face would have made him laugh, if the situation wasn't so serious.

Hawk looked up at the flying delivery drone that hovered above them. "I guess you're not coming." His voice was flat.

The drone did a sideway weaving pattern and then took off into the night. His President's disappointment was evident for only a moment before he pulled himself together.

"All right men, let's see what she gave us." He strode straight over to one of the few picnic tables that were around the clearing.

Max joined him, with Avery close on his heels. After a quick check, Hawk opened the manila envelope and pulled out several pages. His President glanced over the papers quickly, then handed them over.

Avery pressed against his shoulder as she squinted at the pages. He tilted the paper to catch the light of the bonfire so they could both read. The papers appeared to be reports on different individuals.

The top sheet was titled Maria Gomez. It held a picture of a Latina woman, along with her vitals. DOB, height, weight, address, it was all there. Then came more personalized notes, probably from Akula.

Maria is a low level assassin for the family, contracted last year to take out Agent Nathan Chatham. She was chosen because at a distance with bad video she would be mistaken for Avery. Paid for by Mitchel Thomas and recently contracted by Andrey Petrov to kill the guards who had been contracted to kill Avery in order to clean up the loose ends.

On the second page there was a picture of a man Max recognized as one of Petrov's higher ranking soldiers. Timur Sokolov's vital statistics were listed as well.

Timur acted as backup for Maria Gomez during the assassination last year. He is currently partnered with her again with instructions to eliminate her once the job is done.

The last page was a personal letter to Cat.

Hello New Friend,

I've searched through all of both Viktor and Andrey's records. Unfortunately, they are professionals. There was nothing I could find to tie them to what happened to you or your partner. Nothing that would be usable to clear your name.

I have been briefed on the situation as I've been ordered to clean up the mess and remove all loose ends. Andrey wants this embarrassment over and if possible for Viktor to remain in place, as he is useful to the family in his current position.

Understand that taking you out was originally just a job for hire for Mitchel Thomas. He worked closely with my family on many things. When all of the players, but Viktor, were eliminated, the fool decided getting rid of you would reduce the chance his part in the operation would be revealed.

He's had plenty of time to clean up his tracks. I doubt if there's any way now, other than getting a confession, to prove he did any of this.

I wish I had better news for you, but understand at this point, killing you is a point of pride. He is not going to stop. It is my job to make sure this mess doesn't blow back on the family.

I wish you all the best of luck,

Akula

Cat's body tightened against his as she read the note. Her

body practically vibrated with rage.

"So that's it? He gets away with it, and I'm a mess that needs to be *cleaned up*."

Max wrapped his arm around her shoulders and ignored her when she tried to shove him off.

"This is more information. It doesn't mean the end of it. We will keep you safe and Tek and Cami are very good at hunting down a digital trail. With two more names maybe they can find something that connects them."

"Maybe. You mean probably not." Max hated the defeat in her voice.

Hawk stepped forward with Highdive at his side. "All right everybody, let's pack this up. Give us some space."

With that, all the Brothers, except for Highdive and Hawk, started moving what gear they had over to the bikes. They started the process of putting out the bonfire.

"I talked to National earlier," Hawk said.

Max snapped his head up, startled. "Why didn't you tell me earlier?"

"I was hoping we would get better information out of Akula."

"What did they say?"

Hawk ran a frustrated hand through his hair. "They said we can't move against Viktor. It would break our treaty with the Bratva."

"And if he continues to move against my woman?" Max clenched his fists, not liking the way the conversation was going.

Highdive cleared his throat. "The contract on her head started long before she was ever associated with us. We'll defend her but can't take any proactive measures. It will put us all at risk. The best solution we could come up with was for both of you to disappear into one of the other chapters until this is sorted."

His Brother's words were like a punch to the stomach. Max had started out in the Dark Sons Los Angeles chapter, but had been with his Brothers in Denver since its creation. He had never considered leaving them for another chapter.

There was a cold logic in the solution. He could protect both Cat and his Brothers. It didn't mean that the move would not hurt. Every man in the Denver chapter wasn't just his Brother. They were his friends.

He'd spent years with them, getting to know everything about them. Could he walk away and start again? He looked down at Cat and knew he could.

The guilt and fear in her eyes tore him up. He hated that she was going to have to live this way. They would always be on the run from assassins, but it was better than dead.

He gave her a small smile and loved the way her eyes practically lit up with fire. "No." Her denial was a shock. "I'll leave. You guys have done everything you could for me. I appreciate it but I won't let Max get punished for my problems."

Max shook his head. "That's not the way it works, Wildcat." He tilted her chin up and caught her gaze. "You're mine now. There's no turning back from that. I don't care if the two of us have to go to the gates of Hell itself. We are not separating."

The words rang true in his heart, solidifying into a plan in his mind. Yes, these men were his Brothers and his friends. But she was the missing part of him. She was the reason everything he'd done and everything he would do in his life was worthwhile.

They would start over together this time. Build a home they could both enjoy. Together, they would find peace and purpose. And if Viktor kept coming after his woman, he knew hundreds of ways to make problems disappear.

Chapter 27

Giving a woman space is like having all you can eat Mexican. Great for the short term but often extremely painful later that night.

Guilt turned Avery's gut into a swirling mass of tension. Why was he so ready to give up everything for her? She was no one. Just a foster kid who did well in school and managed to get a good job.

She'd even screwed that up. Now this man who had fought his way out of Hell was ready to give up the peace he had found with the family and Brothers, who had his back. Just to keep her safe. It wasn't right.

"So what, you guys would exile Max? I guess they didn't teach you giving in to a bully is wrong, in special ops school."

Hawk's chuckle stoked her anger further. His condescending look didn't help. "Putting down Viktor would be easy, that's not what we are worried about. It's Andrey, his boss."

She knew she shouldn't snap at Hawk, but her frustration made her reckless. "Too big of a fish for you?"

Hawk's eyes were like chips of ice. "Andrey leads over thirty men in Denver alone. Then there is his boss who has access to over a thousand loyal men and even more who can be bought. That doesn't even take into account, Akula, who has found and killed much harder targets than you."

"And you think they would bring them in to attack you if we went after Viktor?"

The scope of everything was making her head hurt. All she wanted was for the truth to come out and for the man to pay for what he had done. Instead, she was stuck in the middle of a game where she didn't understand the rules.

"He is a highly valued operative with access to information they want. Now that we know about him, he might get pulled. But protecting him will be a point of pride for them."

"Why is pride so important to you men?" Avery had seen it time and again when she was undercover. Mexicans, Russians, Italians, all of them seem to put reputation above reality. Max placed a steadying hand on her shoulder. She was surprised he hadn't tried to shut her up already.

Max turned her a little, so she was looking at him. "The only thing that keeps the Underworld from turning into chaos is fear and reputation. If any of us don't enforce our rules or live up to our promises, none of us can work together peacefully."

Hawk gave her a smile, which held too much pity for her tastes. "We've had an uneasy treaty with the Bratva for almost ten years. Without treaties, our Brothers would die in pointless fights over territory. Not just here, but in every chapter across the United States."

It wasn't the fact that she didn't understand what they were trying to say. It was that she didn't want to accept it.

Max squeezed her shoulder. "We aren't superheroes, Cat. There is only so much we can do. Those treaties limit what can or can't be done in our territories. This situation sucks but we still have options as long as we aren't at war."

"So you have to run because of me."

Hawk's sigh held much of the frustration she was feeling. "A smart man knows when it's best to retreat and regroup."

Why were they all willing to let Max pay for her problems? "This is bullshit."

"Wildcat." Max's look was so intense she had to swallow back the words clawing at her throat. "I agree with them. Do I like the fact this dickhead's going to get away with this? No. But if it means keeping you safe and stopping a war that would claim the lives of many of my Brothers," he shrugged, "it's something I'm willing to do."

Avery hated the logic of the whole thing. She wanted to scream and rail against the unfairness of it all. She looked at Hawk and hoped he felt all the anger in her gaze. "Just so I'm clear, you're saying, even if Viktor walked up and threatened me with a gun. If Max took him out, it would create a war."

Hawk nodded. "Yes. Not only with the Bratva, but probably the FBI. We may know that he's dirty, but there is no proof. Maybe, given some time, Cami might be able to find something, or Tek. But until that happens, we can't act."

The fact that Hawk obviously hated what he was saying, as much as she hated hearing it, was only a small salve to her anger.

"What about the other two? The ones who killed my partner."

Hawk's icy glare slid down her spine. "According to Akula, Maria's good as dead. Timur will be harder but we'll find a way."

"I want to be part of that."

She needed to do something. This helpless wave of emotions was tearing at her. A dark part of her resented Max, because he wouldn't give her up. A bigger part of her rejoiced knowing for once someone was choosing her, even though the path was hard.

If they weren't connected, she would be free to do whatever she wanted. The Dark Sons wouldn't have to worry about blowback. They wouldn't have to worry about keeping her alive. It would have been so much easier for them, but because Max loved her they would try to find a way to make it work.

It was crazy thinking about how much she had changed over the last year. She wasn't proud that she no longer cared if Viktor paid through the legal system, or simply with his life. To hell with her freedom. It barely meant anything to her anymore.

The fantasy that she could ride off peacefully into the sunset with Max was just that, fiction. Reality was so much harsher. She was going to have to be on the run for the rest of her life. Dragging him down with her.

Why should Viktor get to roam free?

Max cupped her cheek, making her body want to melt into his. When he touched her, it was tempting to let him make all the decisions. Give over her control. But that wasn't who she was.

"I don't like the thoughts that I see flickering through your eyes, Wildcat. We're going to figure this out together."

There he went again, trying to take on her problems. Didn't he understand? Her love meant she couldn't let him sacrifice his happiness for hers.

She knocked his hand away and immediately missed its warmth and comfort. The hurt she saw in his eyes was like a knife.

He stood straight, and his stoic mask fell back into place. "Nothing's getting finalized tonight. Let's head back to the cabin. We'll talk more there. Figure out what's best for us."

Avery bit back what she wanted to say and slowly walked

over to his bike. To her it was clear what was best for them. The problem would be getting him to accept it.

Her aching heart warred with frustrated anger as she watched Max say goodbye to all of his Brothers. It was like they all knew there was a possibility they would never see him again.

You have to leave him.

The words beat at her heart like a never ending rhythm. She wanted to stay with him, but that meant giving up on making Victor pay right now. The long ride home curled against his muscular back gave her too much time to think.

Would the death of the two people who had killed her partner be enough to satisfy her vengeance? Could she let the man who had orchestrated the entire thing get away with it? If it meant that Max could stay here with his brothers and friends and the two of them could live happily ever after in some sort of fantasy, she might have been tempted. Unfortunately, that wasn't a choice.

Her choices were limited to ruining the life of the man she loved or leaving him and facing her problems on her own. It shouldn't have been a hard choice. She had been facing her problems alone her whole life. But she had never had a person she cared for more than herself.

The time, the fresh air, and the ride, none of it brought her any new ideas. Back inside the cabin she studied the wall, trying to gather her thoughts as Max paced behind her.

There wasn't much in the cabin to distract her from what she needed to say. A coat rack, wall hooks with keys, even the furniture was bare bones. There wasn't a single decoration on the walls to catch her attention.

What were the magic words that would get Max to let her go? Make him understand that she needed to take care of this herself. Maybe then, after everything was resolved, if she was still alive, they could try to be together again.

Avery's eyes burned with tears that she refused to let fall.

"I know you're angry, Wildcat. But you need to see, no matter how awful it is, that the bigger picture is important." His tone was resigned and made her guilt even worse.

"You think I give a shit about the bigger picture?" Avery's throat was tight. "Yeah, I'm pissed because in your version of what's going to happen, Viktor's gonna get away with everything he's doing. He's gonna get to keep his job in the FBI and possibly screw over more innocent people. Leaving him to feed information to our enemies while you and I have to run."

"So what's the problem?"

"The problem is you, Max. You're going to tear apart your life to go on the run with me. And I'm just supposed to be okay with that."

"What would you have me do?"

It was selfish, but what she really wanted was for him to have never given her hope. Even a couple of days ago, she hadn't known half of what she knew now. It might have been naïve, but she had believed there might be a way she could regain her normal life. Finding out that truth had taken that away, shattered what little hope she had left.

"What I don't want is you giving up your life for me." Her voice cracked, and she fought against the tears of frustration that threatened to spill from her eyes.

"I'm not giving up my life. I'm choosing to be with you, spend my life with you." His calm tone did nothing to settle her.

Avery ran a frustrated hand through her hair. "Don't you see that this is wrong? How would you feel if I was giving up, friends, family, everything that made my life good because of something you had done?"

She needed him to understand that she loved him. And because she loved him, she didn't want him sacrificing everything for her.

"I'm not giving up everything that's good in my life. I'm choosing you."

Max grabbed her arms and pulled her close. His mouth crashing down on hers in a passionate kiss. It was so tempting to just give in, to lose herself in this wonderful feeling that happened every time they came together.

But she couldn't.

She tore her mouth away from his, taking three steps back, clenching her fists, trying to hold on to her sanity. "I need time to think."

Avery hated the anger that seemed to boil out of his eyes. "What is that supposed to mean?"

"It means that *I* need to decide what *I'm* going to do next."

"You chose to be with me." He pointed a finger at her that felt like an accusation. "You accepted me. You're my Old Lady. There is no going back from that."

Avery wanted to scream. Everything had become so confusing. When she had accepted him back in that clearing. Everything had seemed so simple. She loved him. He loved her. But it was a fairy tale to believe that that would be enough.

"I love you, Max. But I don't know if I can accept what you and your Brothers decided about what comes next in my life. What you have to give up for me. I can't simply accept what you all planned out."

"And what I think doesn't matter? You're just going to go off and decide our fate by yourself."

Avery snorted. "Isn't that what you did? I wasn't consulted when you decided this plan of us going off hiding for the rest of our lives."

That he was willing to sacrifice so much for her melted a piece of her soul she hadn't realized was frozen. But she didn't think she could let him do that. She sighed and took a small step towards him.

"I need time."

"What the fuck does that mean?" Max talked as if he was forcing each word out through clenched teeth.

"It means I need to be alone." Her eyes caught on the keys that hung on the wall and got an idea. "I'm going to take the truck for a drive and clear my mind."

Where she would go wasn't important. What she needed was the time and distance to be alone to think. She could see him struggle with the idea. Like the war was going on inside his mind. She could only imagine what he was thinking.

"I give you time and you come back and we talk about this. We decide what we're going to do together."

He obviously hated the idea of her going off alone, but was trying to compromise. It warmed her heart that he was going to give her the space she needed, even though she knew it went against every instinct he had.

"Yes."

She watched as too many emotions played over his face for her to understand. Finally, he nodded. Content that he was going to let her go without a fight, she walked over, and grabbed the keys off the hook.

Avery refused to look back as she walked out the door, knowing if she saw the hurt she was causing him in his eyes again, she wouldn't be able to leave. Avery didn't know what she was going to decide. But whatever it was, she was going to find a way to keep Max from throwing away all the happiness that he had so richly earned.

Chapter 28

See, I don't need alcohol to make bad decisions.

Max paced the interior of the cabin and understood what a caged tiger must feel like. Why had he agreed to her driving away? Keeping her here would have been a smarter choice. But he knew his Wildcat couldn't be forced to do anything she didn't want to do. Not and stay the beautiful, vibrant person he loved.

The thought of her out there by herself making decisions that could tear them apart made him want to punch holes in the walls. It was impossible to guess what thoughts were running around in her head. She'd been gone for over an hour. And he had no idea when she was coming back.

He'd started to call her satellite phone almost a hundred times, but stopped himself each time. She wasn't a patient woman and pushing or rushing her would get him the exact opposite reaction of what he wanted.

Her worries were understandable if unwarranted. If their

positions were reversed, he wouldn't have wanted her to walk away from her life for him unless there was no other choice. What she didn't seem to consider was that she was worth it.

The friendships and brotherhood he had developed with the men here in Denver wouldn't end if he left. That was the beauty of the Dark Sons. No matter where he went in the country, he would find men like him.

Individuals who'd chosen loyalty to a brotherhood rather than the arbitrary laws of the country. Men who had sacrificed and given everything to their country only to come back and find they had nowhere that felt like home. Someday they would figure this out and would stop running. Then he would be able to come back with her if they wanted.

And even if that day never came to pass, it didn't matter. Wherever they went, they would make a new home together with a new set of Brothers and their families. Maybe even start a family of their own.

The sound of his phone ringing startled him in the too quiet room of the cabin. Max pulled his phone out of his back pocket. He hoped it would be Avery calling to let him know she was on her way back. To his disappointment the screen displayed the name Tek.

"What's up, Brother?" Max hoped the smart man wouldn't pick up on his anxiety.

"Why the hell is the truck heading into the suburbs of Denver? The same suburbs that Viktor lives in."

Max didn't like Tek's accusing tone, but shock had him muttering a curse. "Avery said she needed to clear her head. I thought she was only planning to ride around the mountain a bit."

"What the hell? You really thought your woman wasn't going to go after Viktor?"

Disappointment and anger warred in his mind. He had stupidly thought they had come to an understanding. That they were going to decide what to do together. But his impulsive Wildcat had obviously decided to take matters into her own hands.

"Yeah, apparently I'm an idiot. Let me call you back." He hung up the phone without waiting for a response.

His hands trembled as he dialed the satellite phone he'd given Avery earlier. Five times he let it ring until it cut off. His anger built like acid against his tongue with each redial.

Max barely resisted the urge to throw his phone against the wall. Why couldn't things ever be simple? He got his breathing under control and dialed Hawk.

"I'm a little busy here. This important?" Hawk's voice sounded strained, and the sounds of multiple people shouting were evident in the background.

Max tried to keep his voice calm. "I'm sorry. Tek called. Apparently Cat took the truck into the city. I think she's going after Viktor."

"Fuck." There was a shuffling noise and a few seconds later the voices in the background faded away. "Val's in labor. We're all about to head out and take her to the hospital."

Dozer and his woman had been trying to have a kid for a long time. Max could only imagine the chaos that vibrant southern woman, who was mother hen to all the Old Ladies, would be stirring up. He hated that his problems would darken their special day even a little.

"I've got to go after her, Hawk."

His President's sigh was loud. "Yeah, I know. We can't back you up officially, but I'll send some Brothers over into the area just in case. I don't want to go to war, Max, but we'll back whatever play you decide."

Relief made Max's knees go weak for a moment. "Thank you."

"Do me a favor and try to stop your woman before she does something stupid."

"Yeah, I hear you." Pride and a renewed devotion to his Brothers filled him with strength.

"Dark Sons for life." Hawk's words were a promise that echoed in his soul.

"Dark Sons for life."

Max ended the call and raced out the door to his bike. He dialed Tek back. Not bothering with a greeting, he said, "Do me a favor and send updates on the location of the truck to my phone. I'm going to see if I can stop her before this all goes sideways."

"Will do. Did you hear about Val?"

"Yeah."

"All right. I'm going to the hospital with Dozer but I'll keep my computer on me and keep you updated."

"Thanks." Max ended the connection and kick-started his bike. If he managed to catch up with Wildcat before it was too late, he was going to tan her ass raw for this stunt.

Max found the truck parked exactly where Tek had said it would be. Unfortunately, Cat was nowhere in sight. The location was about two miles up the road from where he knew Viktor lived on the edge of where the suburbs met a business district.

He could picture what she was doing, as he would have done the same. Sneaking through the residential area on foot would be a lot easier and less remarked on than a strange vehicle parked watching a house. He would have gone on foot using the sidewalks until a block or so before the house, then snuck through the large back yards all these affluent houses seemed to have.

On the way here, he had tried her phone at least a dozen more times. Each time it rang out to voicemail. Max tried it one more time. Sound chirped from inside the cab. Her phone sat forgotten in the center console inside the cup holder.

Max searched the rear tire well until he found the hidden key box. He opened the door and prayed she might have left a clue of what she had planned. Other than the phone, there wasn't anything to find. The gun locker behind the seat still held the rifle and shotgun.

He opened the glove compartment, and he saw the backup handgun was missing. Damn that woman. What was she thinking?

A hundred different images flooded through his mind. His mind focused on the possibilities that she might be dead or needing him. He shook them off. There wasn't enough information to know what was going on.

Did Viktor have men with him at the house? What kind of security did it have? She had broken into the place once, so she knew a lot more than he did.

The Dark Sons had just started gathering information on the man, but Max had been too busy to look over what they had. He shot off a text to Tek. Hopefully, he would have something helpful he could send.

His Brothers would be the ones to suffer if he couldn't clean up this mess. He pictured some of his brothers sitting in the hospital with their families, waiting for the newest member of the Dark Sons to be born. Then he thought of the Brothers Hawk would have sent to him sitting out in the cold nearby, ready to help if he called them. The fall out if she had killed Viktor would be a nightmare for his Club.

Cat didn't understand what that would mean. No one who hadn't seen it could. Innocents wouldn't be spared. And if Viktor had killed her? He would die knowing he started the war because there's no way Max would let him live after that.

The only hope they had was if he found her before she acted. Max looked at his phone. It was after midnight all the men and women of this neighborhood should be asleep. His bike made too much noise for this quiet suburb, but he didn't care.

If Cat heard him, she might hesitate and come find him. Max parked a few blocks away from Viktor's house. There wasn't enough information to make a plan. So he moved from shadow to shadow, trying to do what he thought Cat would have.

The neighborhood was upscale, with each place its own little mini-mansion. They didn't have the amount of property the truly rich would, but it was obvious that each homeowner was trying their best to declare their status. Viktor's house was no exception. A two story modern monstrosity with a circular drive and over manicured lawn. Tall bushes surrounded the property, blocking off view from nosy neighbors. Max's stomach dropped. Unlike its neighbors, lights were visible in all the windows, clearly announcing someone was awake.

Several cars were parked in the drive. He had visitors. Max crept up to the house and settled in the bushes. Fifteen minutes later, he was still trying to decide what to do. There was no noise coming from the house, but not knowing how soundproof the place was, that could mean little.

If there had been a fight, surely the sound would have woken the neighbors. He was near a window and all he could hear was muffled conversation. The front door opened, and he held himself still, counting on the shadows to hide him.

A tall woman stood silhouetted in the doorway. She matched Cat's description of Akula, and she looked pissed.

"Don't be a fool. We can't do this here." Max thanked all the gods that he spoke fluent Russian, as that was what they were speaking.

"What does it matter? I want to watch her die, but it is late. I have no desire to be up all night." The sound of the man's voice

brought with it so many memories. Viktor still sounded like a spoiled, pompous brat after all these years.

"Your weakness sickens me. You would leave potential evidence in your own home because you want a nap? I would have thought you might learn something in the FBI, other than how to whine."

This was the woman who was Hawk's lover? The ice in her voice was enough to shred a man at fifty feet.

"Bitch."

Akula stepped out of the doorway, pulling a woman behind her. They moved down the steps towards the car parked at the top of the circular drive.

"I may be a bitch, but at least I'm not a sniveling puppy begging for scraps from a Papa who will never approve of him."

The woman she practically dragged behind her had her hands bound behind her back, a dark bag over her head as she stumbled on the steps. The sight of the long, dark hair peeking out of the back of the bag set his blood to boiling.

Rational thought flew out of his head as he realized they were planning to take Cat somewhere and kill her. He was too late to stop her from trying to kill Viktor, but he had one chance to give her the opportunity to run. Adrenaline flooded his system, and he burst from cover.

His initial rush startled them, and he was able to knock Akula to the ground and rip Cat out of her grip.

"Run!"

He ripped the hood from her head as he pushed her away from him, turning to face the enemy. He saw recognition on Viktor's face as he charged.

"Grigory?"

Max's shoulder knocked Viktor straight into the doorframe in a blow that staggered them both. Max regretted immediately not going for his gun. Rage was the enemy of any fighter and he had let his blind him.

He wasn't prepared for the five men who poured out of the doorway surrounding him. All his training was for nothing as they piled on him. Within seconds, Max's head was spinning from a blow from behind.

He kicked out, hoping against hope that his reckless charge would give Cat time to escape. Kicks and punches struck him from every direction, and he knew his time was almost up. Another blow to his head had him dropping to his knees.

He looked through the legs of his attackers, hoping to see if Cat had escaped. If she hadn't, at least they would die together.

He was losing the fight to remain conscious. Through blood and bleary eyes, he saw Akula holding a dark-haired woman at knifepoint. Shock was like lightning to his system. That woman wasn't his Wildcat.

Chapter 29

Women are like teabags; we don't know our own strength until we are in hot water.

A very sat in the little diner, staring into her cup of coffee. The place was practically empty, which wasn't a surprise since it was almost one in the morning. Why had she come here? Going anywhere near where Viktor lived was an unnecessary risk. Her original intent had been to drive around the mountain and clear her thoughts.

Instead, she found herself driving back towards the city, towards Viktor's neighborhood. There hadn't been a plan, just instinct. Knowing he was going to get away with everything he had done was a bitter pill. Maybe she had needed to know she could have killed the man before she could come to peace with the decision not to.

Life wasn't fair. Far from it. If she gave into her desire for revenge, there was no way she could guarantee the blowback wouldn't fall on the Dark Sons and their families. The idea of all those people in danger because of something she did wasn't an outcome she could live with.

So for an hour, she had sat, drunk terrible coffee and tried to decide what it was she needed to do. What actions she could live with.

Thank God for the money and gun that she had found in the glove box of the truck. The gun gave her a small sense of security, and the money had given her options other than sitting alone in the car.

It took almost every moment of that time for her temper to cool. For her to be clear-headed enough to look at her actions and words and realize how unfair she had been to Max. Telling him he couldn't go on the run with her was a selfish attempt to protect herself from guilt. Pure ego to think she had the right to make life-altering decisions for him.

It was his life. He had the right to choose what to do with it. Avery had to admit she loved, that for once in her life, someone was choosing her over what was easy. Max was telling her with both words and actions that she was the most important thing to him.

So what did that mean for her? There was no going back to her old life. If he was willing to travel that road with her, then she should accept it. Accept him. Now was the time to build a new life. Together they would find the best way forward. In her heart, she believed Max would help make their new life worth living. Someday she would see Nate's murder avenged, but that didn't have to be today.

It was time to go back and talk to Max. She dropped some money on the table and made the several block trek back to where the truck was parked. When Avery opened the door and the light flickered on. She cursed when she saw her phone sitting in the middle of the console. Her mind had been so caught up in everything that she had forgotten she'd stuck the phone in the cup holder. She settled herself in the driver's seat and picked up the phone.

Forty-two missed calls.

Dread skittered across her skin. Every one of the calls was from Max's number. He would be pissed at her. It had been over two hours. She hoped nothing was wrong, and he had simply gotten tired of waiting for her to return.

It was a thirty-minute drive back to the cabin. Did she want to call him back now? Or wait, so they could talk in person. It was tempting to put off his lecture. But that many missed calls seemed excessive if he was worried. Her stomach dropped. Something must have happened.

She hit the button to dial him back with a sinking feeling in her heart. After three rings, someone picked up.

"Your man is an idiot." Akula's voice caused her throat to tighten in shock.

"Akula?" The name was a strangled squeak and Avery cleared her throat.

"Yes, my new friend. It's me."

Why the hell would the crazy Russian woman have Max's phone? "Where's Max?"

"I'm afraid I have to tell you, your man is currently being tortured to find out your location."

Chills spiked across her spine. Had someone found the cabin and taken him? Who took him? How did Akula get his phone? Avery punched the steering wheel, and the pain in her hand allowed her to focus. This assassin talking so casually about Max being tortured didn't seem to understand how her words might affect her.

"I don't understand."

"I'm guessing you ran away from him." Shame flushed Avery's cheeks at the woman's accurate guess. "He must have thought you were going after Viktor. So, like a fool on a white horse, he charged in to save you. Unfortunately for him, his timing was crap. He mistook Maria Gomez for you and rushed in blindly."

The more Akula talked, the more confused Avery grew. "So he rescued Maria Gomez?"

"No. Though he made a valiant attempt at it."

"So you and Viktor have him."

"Viktor has him. I'm just the muscle his boss sent in to oversee things."

It was hard to understand this woman. Whose side was she on? "So what? I turn myself in and you let him go. Is that the deal?"

Akula's laughter was deep and warm, even over the phone. "Please tell me you're not as much a fool as your man. If someone was to offer you that deal I hope you wouldn't believe that they would hold up their end."

Avery clenched the steering wheel in frustration. Her jaw hurt as she clenched her teeth in an attempt not to shout, "I don't suppose I would."

"Good. Your man seems to have some personal history with Viktor. Hawk should have told me this."

Max was being tortured, and this woman wanted to talk about information sharing? Anger caused her body to tremble. She tried to placate the only person with the information she needed. "I don't know if Hawk knew."

"Perhaps. Either way, Viktor seems set on breaking your man personally. So he has him holed up in a warehouse outside of the city. Luckily for you, he is planning on taking his time."

Luckily? Vivid images of Max tied up, beaten, and bloody filled her mind. Part of her training to become an undercover agent had been learning what might happen to you if you were ever uncovered. She knew what had happened to her at Mitchel's compound was only child's play compared to what might have happened. She'd seen pictures of torture and the thought of that happening to the man she loved enraged her.

"You're telling me this… why?" The woman had to have some sort of angle other than gloating over Max's predicament.

"Because I really am in town to do a job. That job is to clean up this mess. If that means I can kill Viktor, weaken and embarrass Andrey, and help Hawk all at the same time, even better."

Did she dare trust this woman? More to the point, did she have a choice? She could call Max's Brothers, but would they be in time? Probably not. It was going to be a leap of faith either way.

"What do you want me to do?"

"Good. You are as smart as I hoped. We shall meet and I will share with you my plan. If you follow my directions exactly, maybe, and I mean maybe, you and your white knight might come out of this alive."

Chapter 30

Roses are red skies are blue, out of my five fingers the middle one is for you.

The shock of cold water forced Max out of the dark grip of unconsciousness. His skull felt like sharp knives were attempting to Julienne his brain. The rest of his body throbbed with the deep ache of bruises that would take weeks to heal. What the hell had happened?

Max sorted through his memories, trying to parse through what had happened at Viktor's house. Pain swirled, and he tried to focus. From what he could remember, he was pretty sure it was sheer luck he wasn't dead. He opened his eyes and winced against the light.

The room he was in was a bare space that lacked furniture. High ceilings meant it was probably inside a warehouse. He sat forward and his shoulders strained. His hands were held in place by rope tying him to the thick metal chair. He moved his legs and felt the frustrating bite of rope holding him there as well.

Immobile and injured wasn't the best condition to wake up in. Timur, one of Andrey's soldiers, stood by the door like a guard dog. His presence meant that Andrey would soon be involved and if he wasn't careful, his Brothers would pay for his reckless actions. The only other person in the room for the moment was Viktor. He loomed a few feet away, an all too familiar smile on his face.

"Good, you're awake." Viktor tossed aside the metal bucket he was holding with a laugh. "My old friend Grigory. Can you imagine how surprised I am to see you?" The sound of the man's snide merriment brought back unpleasant memories of when Max would have to stand by and listen as the asshole beat and tortured helpless people for his amusement.

His time in Russia was some of the more common memories that still replayed, even now, in his nightmares. One might think that killing people would be what haunted him, but he didn't regret his kills. He only regretted having to act as a silent witness and friend to this sadistic man. There was nothing he could ever do to make up for his sins.

Wallowing in the past wouldn't help him now. He needed to figure out how to play this. Viktor had outwardly changed since Max had known him as a young man, but the core of him would be the same. The ego, need to be accepted, and the sadistic drive to harm others to make himself feel strong was at the core of his personality. If he was to have any hope of controlling the situation, Max would have to push Viktor's buttons and see what triggers the man still held.

"Long time no see." Max enjoyed Viktor's annoyed scowl.

The man leaned forward as if sharing a secret. "Do you know I mourned for you?" He stood and spat to the side. "My friend and loyal men, killed by a car bomb set by my enemies.

I got vengeance for you. The things I did to the men I thought responsible are still legend."

"I was never your friend." Max knew exactly what had happened after his fake death. He had spent months setting the whole thing up so that not only would it kill the strongest of Viktor's soldiers, but start a war between the two families.

"Apparently not. What were you then? A spy?"

He was surprised Viktor guessed the truth so quickly. It was tempting to rub the smug man's face in how thoroughly he had been fooled. Years had passed and the other spies he had worked with over in Russia were probably not still active, but Max couldn't take that risk. Giving up his old identity for the sake of gloating would be childish. He needed to spin a tale that had a chance of being believed.

Max spoke in Russian, the old accent easy to remember. *"No, I was a boy trying to make my way in a hard world. You were my meal ticket."* Max let all the disgust he felt show on his face. *"No matter how hard I made my heart, eventually, even what you paid me wasn't enough. I couldn't stomach being around your sickness anymore. So I found my own freedom. Escaped right under your nose."*

Viktor strode up to him and hit him across the face with a back-handed blow that split his lip. The pain that lanced through Max's cheek was much greater than the blow should have caused. The fight earlier must have fractured something in his head. The room spun, and his vision dimmed for a moment. A concussion meant he needed to be careful if he wanted to stay aware.

Viktor's breath hissed over his ear as he spoke. *"You taught me how to do many of those things that you claim made you sick. Showed me the best way to hurt people, make people fear me. Don't sit there like some sanctimonious priest and pretend you're better than me."*

Max coughed to clear his throat, bothered by the fact he hadn't even tracked the man coming so close to him. He clenched his fists and tried to get his eyes to focus. *"I may have taught you how to do the things your father wanted. But you were the one who enjoyed them. Not me."* It was a risk, pissing this man off, but every anger inducing word was necessary if he was going to get Viktor to believe the new story and not to go digging into the past.

If by some miracle Max survived this encounter, he needed to give himself the best chance of not having his secrets uncovered. If he had only taken the time to think earlier, he wouldn't even be here. It was an amateur mistake letting his emotions take over his actions. He needed to remember his training, who and what he was. Those skills were the only way he was going to survive.

Much to Max's disappointment, Viktor stood and seemed to rein in his temper. "So you left the family, came in the US, and joined a bunch of bikers."

"Yes."

Viktor threw back his head and laughed as if Max had said something hilarious. "I'm not a fool to believe your lies again. Akula is right now finding out who you really are. Mad Max." Viktor flicked the name patch on his cut. "You will tell me where that bitch who keeps escaping me is."

Hope flared in Max's chest. Viktor hadn't caught Cat. Hopefully she would contact his Brothers, they would keep her safe for him, even if he didn't escape. Options raced through his mind. Whose side was Akula on? She had helped Cat the other day, but was there any way she would help him now?

He didn't see her around, but she might be outside this room. Max prayed she wasn't actually reporting to the Bratva about his miraculous return from the dead. It was a faint hope. Hawk had told him that while she might help if she could get away with it, her first loyalty was to her family.

Max glared at his captor. "I'm not going to tell you anything."

"I think you will. I think you will break like a spineless

coward. Then I will take joy in killing her and ruining the lives of anyone you care about while you are broken and helpless. Only then when you are begging me to die will I end your suffering."

It would be foolish to believe that he couldn't be broken. Given enough time and a skilled torturer, everyone would eventually say whatever was needed to make it stop. His only comfort was that he didn't have the information Viktor wanted. By the time he broke she would be long gone, and his Brothers would have taken steps to protect both her and themselves.

"Nothing to say? That's okay. I wouldn't want you to make this too easy. I'm going to enjoy hurting you. Resist. It makes the begging later that much sweeter." The punch to his stomach made bile rise up into his throat as the already bruised muscles absorbed the blow. "Where is the girl?"

Max laughed, choking back the urge to vomit. "You were always stupid. I obviously don't know. Otherwise, I wouldn't have tried to free whoever that woman was at your house. She took off yesterday morning and I haven't seen her since."

Surviving interrogation without helping the enemy was like a game. He needed to mix truth with lies from the beginning. The more confusion he could create now, the more likely it was that Viktor wouldn't be able to separate truth from fiction. The key was giving away things that didn't matter and spinning believable stories.

Viktor pulled out a knife and smiled as he tested the point. "I had wondered about that. It was cruel of you to give Maria hope she might live."

Maria? Akula's data had said she was the one who had killed Cat's partner. It made a sick sort of sense that he had mistaken her for Cat since the woman had been chosen for the job because of her surface resemblance to his woman. He had made the same mistake the cops had and assumed the two women were the same person.

"So Maria's dead?"

"Of course, she had fulfilled her purpose. She wasn't family, only a hireling. With Avery out and free I couldn't take the chance that she could be used to prove her innocence."

Max wanted to roll his eyes, but kept his face blank. Viktor always loved to brag about his own genius. He'd never once taken into consideration how that made him look. It didn't make him seem important or smart, just petty and cruel.

"Funny to hear you using that word, family. Does that mean they are pretending to accept you now? I seem to remember things differently. You were only another one of their pets. How did you get your father to acknowledge you?"

Rage flared in his eyes, letting Max know the man was still considered a bastard. Viktor lashed out, this time punching Max in the chest. The crack of a rib unmistakable in the quiet room. Max took several shallow breaths, trying to not let out a groan of pain.

"I have you to thank for my rise in the family. If you hadn't taught me such a good American accent, I would never have been able to infiltrate the FBI. Andrey hand-picked me for this job so it doesn't matter what my weakling of a father says."

Big words that were obviously lies. This man was still a boy under his tough exterior, trying to get his father's approval. The knowledge that the stupid game he had used to distract Viktor had gone so wrong was infuriating. Teaching him accents was supposed to be a way to pick up women at the bar. Pretend to be American to lure in easy pussy and keep Viktor from playing more deadly games.

Max had never thought it would lead to this. He had created a spy to be turned against his own country. In a way, that meant he had been responsible for everything going on.

"Does that bother you? Knowing that something you taught me is going to secure my place within the family? Two more years and I'll be able to shake off this identity and take my rightful place."

Max shook his head. "You really believe they're going to accept you? From what I've heard, you are a laughingstock. Hell, you botched a simple clean-up job, and you think they'll trust you in the inner circle?"

Rage flushed Viktor's face, and he began raining blows down on Max's torso. His head was spinning and his heartbeat pulsed in his ears. Maybe he wouldn't survive this, but he was proud he hadn't betrayed anyone.

It took Max a few seconds to realize the blows had stopped. His ears rang, and he tasted copper on his tongue.

"Find out what's going on," Viktor's shout felt muffled.

His breath was harsh and Max tried to listen to whatever it was that had caught the Russian's attention. It took a few seconds to realize the thuds he was hearing wasn't his pulse. It's funny, civilians think suppressed fire is silent. As if people around you could fire and you would never know. While it's not as loud as unsuppressed fire, it's still has a distinctive sound. There was a lot of it going on somewhere nearby.

Tamir turned to the door and pulled his weapon. As soon as he opened the door, blood spattered across the wall and floor behind him. The large man crumpled backwards to the floor.

A woman stepped through the door, and for a moment Max thought he was dreaming, hallucinating even. His Wildcat stood framed in the doorway, the darkness of night behind her, and an assault rifle with a suppressor pressed to her shoulder. She looked like a goddess of wrath. He didn't know who was more surprised in the next moment, him or Viktor, as she turned and without a single word, fired.

The shot took the Russian in the shoulder and knocked

him to the ground. Cat stepped forward, and he realized she was still in her same outfit from earlier. The short jean skirt and scoop neck shirt a strange contrast to the military style weapon she was wielding.

His Wildcat was here.

Max blinked, trying to clear his vision. How could she be here?

"Hey, honey, I've come to rescue you." The smile on her face made his heart soar.

Dear God, he loved this woman. Max looked down to see Viktor struggling to pull his own gun from his position on the ground. Without a pause, Cat raised her rifle and emptied three shots into him. The man fell motionless to the floor.

Her smile was magnetic as she continued to move forward. She stopped to check Viktor's pulse and gave a small nod before she slung her weapon onto her back. Cat put her hands on her hips and gave him a saucy wink.

"Well, don't you look a mess."

He laughed out of pure shock, but cut it off almost immediately because of the pain in his ribs. This whole situation was going to be a nightmare for his Club, but he couldn't help but feel joy knowing she was alive and free.

She bent down and gave him a kiss on the cheek. She whispered into his ear. "Just a bit more drama to go. I need you to roll with it and remember everything's going to be all right."

Max had no idea what she meant, but trusted she had a plan to get them out of here safely. The door opened and Akula stood in the opening, dressed all in black. She held an assault rifle at her shoulder.

Had she helped Cat get him free? How is she going to explain this to the Bratva? Cat had started to untie his ropes so he almost missed the double cross. Time froze as the Assassin raised her weapon and pointed it straight at Cat's back.

His scream of warning was too late as three quick shots echoed in the room. Cat let out a groan and his heart shattered as blood splattered onto his body before she collapsed onto the floor. He barely took in the red that splattered the floor as he strained against his bonds.

"You bitch!" he screamed, his throat raw with agony.

"I am really tired of people calling me that."

He lurched against the chair and tried to rip free of his bonds. She hadn't moved from the doorway. His chair rocked and she raised her rifle back to her shoulder. Pain exploded across his chest. And he felt the wetness splattering against his face as his chair tipped over backwards.

Pain wracked his body and soul. He had trouble breathing in the new position, his arms pinned underneath the chair. He didn't care. Cat was dead. What was the point anymore? The sound of several more shots filled the room, but he barely noticed. The sound of the woman's boots as she crossed the floor was like a countdown. She was going to finish him off. In his last moments, he had only one wish.

To see Cat one last time before he joined her in death.

Chapter 31

Life is a shitshow so smile for the cameras.

Avery struggled to remain still while she listened to Max's shouts of pain and heartbreak. Cursing Akula in her mind, she fumed. If the woman had given her one more minute before acting, she could have let him in on the plan and saved him from the emotional pain. She could only imagine what was going through his head. Making him believe she was dead was cruel, but breaking character now would destroy the fiction they were attempting to create.

Akula's plan was insane, even if it seemed to be working. The two of them had taken out the two sentries on the way in. Then created enough noise to cause Viktor to send out Timur. That was where the show for the cameras had begun. Killing Timur and Viktor was easy after she saw what they had done to Max.

Once the man who had destroyed her life was dead, Akula had said the only way to avoid war would be for both her and

Max to appear to die. Somehow the woman had found a real-istic paintball rifle to use as a prop in their video drama. From the ache in her back, Avery knew she was going to have three deep welts from where the unusual ammunition had hit her. The sound of Akula's footsteps approaching meant she had disabled the cameras. It was tempting to move, but as promised, Avery remained still.

"Cameras are disabled. Get your man to the van while I set this place to blow."

Avery popped up to her knees, desperate to see how badly Max had been hurt in the fall. He had already been in rough shape before getting knocked back in his chair. She hoped that falling onto his arms hadn't broken any bones. As she turned to see Max, Akula handed her a knife. He was slack-jawed as he stared up at her from his position on the floor. Her throat tightened as she saw tears shimmering in his eyes.

"You're alive." His voice was a harsh croak.

She gave him a small smile that she hoped told him how sorry she was for making him believe she was dead. "I told you it would all work out. I didn't have time to tell you more."

He was too heavy to pull his chair upright without first getting him free. The ropes around his wrists were her first task. She hoped to get the pressure off before any more damage was done to his arms. The moment his arms were no longer pinned, he clutched her to his chest in a crushing grip.

Max squeezed, and her breath came out in a rush. He looked down into her eyes with wonder. "How? I mean why?"

Avery pulled back and placed a gentle kiss on his lips. There was so much to say. She didn't even know where to start.

"Explain to him later. Get him to the van now." Akula was right, but she knew her man would be desperate for answers.

"We have to hurry, Max if this is going to work." Avery pulled out of his grip, which she didn't think she could have done if he wasn't so hurt. She quickly cut the rope securing his legs and helped him to stand. "Trust me a bit longer."

Max nodded as his body swayed. Fear twisted her guts as she steadied him. How badly was he hurt? She wanted to examine every inch of him to make sure he would be all right, but there would be time for that later. For now, they needed to get to the van.

From the way he moved, his legs didn't seem to be injured, but his balance was off and he winced with every movement. She guided him out of the room and down the hall to the loading dock where they had backed up Akula's van. Avery opened the back doors and pulled Max inside and down to the floor against the side panel.

The van was designed for cargo, not passengers, with a solid panel blocking access to the driver. A small vent allowed air to pass through, but with no windows, it would be impossible for anyone to see them once the doors were closed. She flicked on the dome light before shutting them.

Avery grabbed the first-aid kit they had stashed in there before kneeling. Max had closed his eyes and she could only imagine the pain that was causing the tight lines in his face. She touched his hand and emotion rushed through her.

They had done it. She had saved Max, and they were almost out of here. Akula's over the top plan was actually working. Desperation had been her only motivation to agree to any of this. She loved him so much, and would have risked anything to save him.

His eyes opened, and she swore she saw the same emotion in his gaze.

She shook her head and tried to get back on task. "Do you think anything's broken?" There wasn't much she could do if there was, but evaluating how much medical help he would need would be a factor in any future plans.

"Who cares? You're alive, that is all that matters."

She gave him a stern look. "No, it's not. I want to know everything they did to you."

"Why? They are already dead. Vengeance accomplished." His chuckle was soft and morphed quickly into a groan.

"Max!"

He raised his hand slowly and cupped her cheek. "I've got a few ribs that might be broken. Bruises that make it hard to move and my head is spinning so badly, I'm not positive this isn't a hallucination."

She gripped his hand, loving how he wasn't hiding his emotions from her. "I'm real."

"So what happens now?"

The rest of the plan was complicated, and she hoped he would agree to it. "We need to stay hidden for her plan to work. I promised her that no matter what happens we won't let anyone know we're alive until she lets us out of the van and has time to explain things."

"Does she think someone's going to come before then?"

"It's possible. She said either Bratva or your Brothers might show up. There are contingency plans for either event. She swore she has a way for us to stay together. One that won't start a war or have people hunting either of us."

She could see Max's doubt in his eyes, but he paused, hopefully thinking about what she had said. "You trust her?"

That was a complicated question. That held a lot of 'What other choice do I have' in the answer. "She's gone out on a limb for us and so far she hasn't done anything to betray us. So, yes, at least for now, I trust her."

"Okay, then I'll follow your lead."

His faith in her meant everything. She wanted to kiss him and show him just how wonderful she thought he was, but it wasn't the time or place. In his condition, it would probably be weeks before she could really show her appreciation of his trust.

Avery used the medical scissors to cut away Max's shirt. His torso was a mess of black and purple bruising. Even his stomach was mottled with color. Avery bit her lip. If he had internal bleeding, there wasn't much she could do about it. She would have to watch him closely and hope he stayed conscious.

On a positive note, now that they were settled down in to the back of the van, his breathing didn't appear labored. Honestly, if she didn't see the evidence of his injuries on his skin, she wouldn't have guessed he was injured. Other than the bruising, he only had minor cuts. The kind that were only small splits in the skin caused by a hard blow. The first-aid kit wouldn't do him much good.

"Do you want me to wrap your ribs?" She held up the large ace bandage.

Max grimaced. "No. A few of them might be more than just fractured. It's not worth the risk."

"All right. Boys and girls, it's time to go." Akula's voice came from the front of the van.

Avery sat down next to Max in the hope she could help him remain steady while the vehicle moved. After a minute or two of bumpy travel on the gravel parking lot, the ride smoothed out. At the same time, she heard the unmistakable rumble of a lot of bikes as they surrounded them.

"Your Brothers better not mess this up for me." Akula's voice was filled with frustration. "You two remember your promise and stay quiet."

Max raised his eyebrow, and Avery nodded at him. She hoped he would keep his word. The plan hinged on everyone believing the two of them had died.

The vehicle came to a stop. Avery stilled as she listened to Akula's confident voice from up front. "I will only talk to Hawk. Tell those boys not to go closer to that warehouse. It's about to explode."

There were muttered shouts from the people surrounding the van.

"Turn off the van." Sharp's voice was unmistakable even through the small vent.

"No. Get Hawk. Don't go close to the warehouse. I've given you simple instructions so you should be able to understand them."

A few seconds later, the sound of Hawk's frustrated voice was clear. "What the hell is going on, Alena? Where is my man?"

Akula's name was Alena? Avery wondered if it was her real name or another alias?

"I've missed you too. Darling."

It was hard to imagine anyone willing to talk to the scary man who was Hawk in such a flippant tone, but the assassin had ovaries of steel.

"I'm not in the mood for your games. Where is Max?"

"He's dead. So is his woman." She said the words as if she was talking about the weather and it was boring. This was the part of the plan that Avery hated. Max glared at her and for a moment she thought he was going to blow their cover. The sound of the explosion hit a second before the van rocked from the shock wave.

"Is that your work?" Hawk's tone was tight.

"The warehouse maybe. Your man and his woman, no. Now, unless you want to deal with the police, you and I will go somewhere alone and I will catch you up."

"I'm not going anywhere with you alone," Hawk growled.

"You don't trust me?" Avery swore she heard genuine hurt in Akula's voice.

"Not after last time."

"I told you I didn't know they would be there."

"I'm not arguing about this."

The back and forth between the two of them was so

natural that Avery was starting to believe they had a much longer history than she originally thought. If she hadn't known better, she would have thought the two of them were an old married couple.

"Fine, pick three of your men who you trust. I will follow you to somewhere you choose. Otherwise, the deal's off and we can wait for the cops."

"I don't think you want to be here when the police get here anymore than I do."

She snorted. "I'm a friend of the owner. You're the President of an Outlaw MC. I tell them you came and blew up this place. Who do you think they'll believe?"

Hawk's growl was almost a roar. "What the hell happened to my Brother?"

"I told you," ice filled her words, "I'll explain somewhere else. I'll follow you wherever you want to go as long as it is close and there are only four of you."

"You better not be screwing with me."

"I'm not. Though we might be able to arrange that for later."

There was a loud slam against the side of the vehicle that made Avery jump and knock into Max. He groaned, the sound loud, and she put her hand over his mouth to muffle it. She tried to hold still and hoped Hawk hadn't heard anything. The silence stretched, and she held her breath.

"Fine. Follow me."

Chapter 32

If the decision was easy then it wasn't really a choice.

When the back doors of the van swung open before Akula even turned off the engine, Max wasn't surprised to see Hawk's concerned face. He'd hoped his President had heard him back here earlier. It had been too good an opportunity to pass up when Avery fell against him to make a noise loud enough to be heard. Neither of the women would have accused him of breaking their deal. He wasn't sure what the Russian woman had planned. But whatever it was, he knew his Brothers could be trusted, and he wouldn't have agreed to any plan that kept them in the dark.

"Damn, Brother, you look like shit." Hawk's face was shadowed in the small illumination of the van, but his smile was bright.

Avery was tense and looked ready to fight. Max gripped her hand and hoped she would understand they were safe. Whatever was going to happen, they would face it together.

"Yeah, but it beats being dead."

The front door to the van slammed, and he heard Akula coming around to the back.

"Well, you've figured out my surprise."

Hawk snorted and shook his head. "You may be a cold-hearted bitch Alena, but the moment you told me my brother was dead that way, I knew you were lying."

She leaned back against the open door and waved a hand dismissively. "Yes, yes. The all-powerful Hawk knows all. I suppose now it's story time." She clapped her hands. "Right, you two. Out of the back so we can talk."

Max did his best not to show just how much he hurt as he and Cat slid out of the van. Everything down to his fingers ached, and he was sure at least two of his ribs were fractured. Fortunately, standing was actually more comfortable than sitting on the floor of a vehicle. He took a slow breath to steady himself.

It could have been so much worse. His head still throbbed, but he took it as a good sign that his vision seemed to be back to normal. The night air was cool against his skin since Cat had cut open his shirt. His leather cut hadn't been designed for warmth, so he hoped this conversation wouldn't take too long.

Cat slid under his arm, doing her best not to touch his chest, but he suspected she needed the comfort of his touch as much as he needed hers. Max didn't have the heart to tell her, every time she took a deep breath, he could feel it in his ribs. Pain wouldn't keep him from keeping her at his side.

Sharp, Hannibal, and Ink approached, their boots scuffing against the dirt. He was glad to see them as they gave him chin lifts. Max recognized the scenic rest stop they were parked in. It was a good choice, far enough off the road to hide them from passing cars but open enough that motorcycles would have an advantage if she had tried to break away. The sounds of sirens were muffled somewhere out in the darkness, so the warehouse wasn't too far away.

He was embarrassed to admit he had lost all track of time because of the pain of sitting during the bumpy ride. Akula closed the doors, and all light from the vehicle was cut off. The night was bright with an almost full moon, so once their eyes adjusted, it was easy to see everyone.

Max turned to Akula, tired of the waiting game. "So what's your grand plan?"

She looked over at Hawk, and Max would have sworn she looked sad. "The relationship between the Bratva and the Dark Sons has always been tenuous at best. Here in Denver, more than anywhere else, it would take very little to destroy the truce."

Hawk nodded. "I know Andrey hates me. He hasn't been subtle."

"Yes, well he wanted more than anything to use this as a spark to set off a war."

Cat perked up. "Wanted?"

"Yes. He was encouraging Viktor to go after you, even after he knew Max had claimed you. He was not happy when I told him that Viktor had kidnapped Max in order to draw you out, Avery."

Sharp crossed his arms. "And he believed you?"

"Yes, Viktor has never been the brightest bulb in the pack. My orders were to find them both and try to clean up the mess before the Dark Sons found out."

Max couldn't believe Andrey would think that would work. "What were you supposed to do?"

"Kill you and make sure the body was never found so there would be no proof that Viktor had acted first."

"So what was the point of all the drama back at the warehouse?" Max was still angry about what she had done. The terror he had felt in those minutes when he thought Avery was dead would stay with him for all of his days.

"Viktor had to die to sell the lie. But without proof other than my word and yours his death would have been enough for Andrey to convince the rest of the family to go to war with the Dark Sons. The only way to avoid that was to give them a life for life."

"Fine, but why have her kill him and then pretend to kill both of us?" Max had been part of plenty of twisted situations in his life but this woman's twisted plotting had his head spinning.

"I killed her and shot you, so here we have a choice. I can either say that I killed her, but managed to save you. And to the family the slate will be even. Or I can say I had to kill both of you. And Hawk can conveniently get one of his hackers to pull the video feed putting Andrey squarely in his debt."

"You want me to use video proof that you killed my people to blackmail Andrey? Won't that put you in a bad position?" Hawk sounded appalled at the idea of Akula being used as a bargaining chip.

Her smile was gentle as she responded. "My face never made it on to any camera. All you will have is proof that your man was kidnapped and then killed when his woman tried to free him. Either way, she needs to disappear for at most a year. But your Brother can stay in Denver if he wants to."

Max felt Avery's sharp intake of breath. It was tempting to make the choice himself. But that's where he had gone wrong before. There was no way he wasn't going to go with her wherever she went. But maybe if he made her part of the decision this time, things would turn out differently.

Cat spoke up. "Why would I only have to disappear for a year?" Max startled and realized he had missed an important part of what Akula had said.

"You would still have to hide from law enforcement, but

things are happening within my family. Andrey won't be an issue for much longer."

"What's going on?" Hawk's question was a barked demand that had Akula glaring at him.

"Family business and none of yours," she hissed back at him.

It was easy to tell this was going to escalate if it continued. While It was fascinating to watch, Max wanted time to work things out with Cat. He looked around at everyone. "Can you guys give us a minute?"

Max smirked as Hawk pulled Akula off in one direction and motioned for his Brothers to go in the other. It was clear that the two of them had a lot more to discuss than just this decision. Once he and Avery were alone, he turned to her.

Even in the dim light, she was so beautiful. Everything she had done today for him made her that much more fascinating. He wanted to spend the rest of his life with this woman. But he knew if it wasn't her choice, she would never really be his. He needed her to be completely on board with whatever they did.

She tilted her chin up at him in a defiant gesture that made him want to smile. "Do you want to stay? I can understand, if you do. I wouldn't be in danger anymore and I'm sure your brothers would help me start a new life somewhere else." Her words had come out in a rush that was filled with nervous energy.

Max bit back the urge to growl at her. "Is that what you want?"

He could hear her swallow before she spoke. "No, it's not." She looked up at him and the moon reflected in her eyes. "While you were busy getting kidnapped, I was at a crappy diner, getting my head on straight. I want you, Max. I want to spend every day of the rest of my life with you. But it's you who has a choice, not me."

Ignoring the pain in his ribs. He gripped her face in his hands and kissed her. He poured all his love and desire, every bit of the happiness he felt in hearing those words into the kiss. He loved her. He bit back a groan as she melted into him and pressed against his chest. Not caring how much it hurt, he deepened the kiss, needing to show her how much she meant to him.

He pulled back and pressed his forehead against hers. "I love you. I love your strength. I love when you're a brat. I don't want to spend a single day of my life not getting to experience all the wild and crazy things that are you."

Her smile was everything he could hope for. It was something he prayed he would see every day for the rest of his life.

"Let's go tell them what we decided."

Epilogue

I promise to always be by your side… or under you… or on top.

The last few weeks at the cabin while Max recovered had been like a dream. Cat was almost sad they would be leaving their little mountain hideaway. The location was secluded, but it was still too big of a risk that they might be found. She stood on the porch, taking in the beauty of the forest for a final time.

The creaking of the front door broke into her mental wandering, and she smiled back over her shoulder at Max. All his bruises had healed, and he was back in fighting form. He had proved that to her very thoroughly yesterday when he had hunted her through the woods. Now, the only wounds on his body were her nail marks on his back.

Max wrapped his arms around her, pulling her against his body in a warm embrace. She leaned her head back on his shoulder and wondered how she had gotten so lucky to find a man who fulfilled her every fantasy.

"Almost ready to go?" He nuzzled her cheek and nipped playfully at her ear.

She laughed. "Not if you keep doing that."

He spun her around and took her mouth in a kiss that sent her heart racing. She groaned as he pulled back, and she tried to pull herself together. He always blamed their insatiable need for one another on her, but she thought it was his fault. Who could resist someone who treated them like both a precious gift and a valued partner?

"Did you say all of your goodbyes?"

She laughed. "Yes. I still can't believe they snuck up here."

They had been woken this morning when Cami and Val had burst into the cabin like a pair of tornados carrying a baby. It had warmed her heart that the two women had apparently staged a breakout from the compound to come up and say goodbye and let her meet Val's baby.

"Dozer is going to give her hell when she gets back to the compound."

"He should have known better than to try to keep her confined after the doctor gave her the all-clear." Cat raised her eyebrow, daring him to disagree.

Max shook his head. "Not my place to judge. That is between them."

"Brinley is a beautiful baby. She's going to be breaking hearts in no time."

"You mean Dozer's going to be breaking heads."

Cat rested her head on Max's chest. "I still can't believe what Cami did for me."

"I can. That woman is a miracle worker with a computer."

"Yes, but to hack birth records and social services to create a twin for me?" The level of trouble the woman had gone to was amazing.

Inside, Cat had every piece of documentation she would need to create a real life without fear of ever getting caught.

Catherine Perez, twin of Avery Perez, was just as real as any person could be. Cami had not only created a digital trail, including social media, and faked pictures of the 'twins' but she had doctored a will and gotten all of Avery's assets and death benefits transferred over to accounts in Catherine's name. The story was they had been separated in foster care but had reconnected later in life. If someone ever recognized her, she had the perfect cover story.

"She likes you. All the Old Ladies do."

"I like them too. I'm going to miss them. Speaking of that, are you going to tell me where we are going?"

Max ran a hand down her cheek. "I was thinking we would head down to Texas for a bit. We don't have to settle right away."

"If Akula was right, would you want to come back here?"

Her whole body shivered as he ran his hands down her back and cupped her ass. "I don't know. I kind of like the idea of traveling with my woman for a while."

"Your woman, huh?" She bit his chest. Two could play the teasing game.

"Are you packed, Wildcat?" His voice held the sexy growl that she loved so much.

"Yup." She slid her hand around to cup his cock which was pushing against her stomach.

His growl had things tightening low in her body. She gasped as he spun her roughly around and held her back firmly against his chest. He moved them so she was facing directly at the stairs of the porch, the path into the woods clearly visible.

"If we're going to make the hotel I planned on staying at tonight…" He spoke softly into her ear.

"Yes?"

"We have two hours before we need to leave." His hand

brushed over her tight nipples sending jolts of pleasure through her.

"What do you think we should do with that time?"

"I know what you should do."

Cat bit her lip. "What's that?"

"Run!"

Ann Jensen

I'm a snarky Jersey Woman who dreamed of one day becoming an Author. I write Romance with bigger than life characters who have to dodge every obstacle I gleefully throw in their paths. Somehow my characters also find time for steamy fun on their way to their HEAs.

I'm an avid reader, engineer, photographer, and a proud Bi woman. My life is a journey that I hope never stops in one place too long. I fill it with love and laughter whenever possible and when I can't, I pull out my clue by four and use it with deadly precision.

https://annjensenwrites.com/

Dark Sons Motorcycle Club
Saved by the Dark
Lost in the Dark
Caught in the Dark
Undercover In the Dark

Blushing Books

Blushing Books is the oldest eBook publisher on the web. We've been running websites that publish steamy romance and erotica since 1999, and we have been selling eBooks since 2003. We have free and promotional offerings that change weekly, so please do visit us at http://www.blushingbooks.com/free.

Blushing Books Newsletter

Please join the Blushing Books newsletter
to receive updates & special promotional offers.
You can also join by using your mobile phone:
Just text BLUSHING to 22828.

Every month, one new sign up via text messaging will receive
a $25.00 Amazon gift card, so sign up today!

www.ingramcontent.com/pod-product-compliance
Lightning Source LLC
Chambersburg PA
CBHW030253200626
46816CB00002BA/629